... 'U

...er
...p
...y

...thrall, and illuminate. The world spins on, yet in varying ways Cuba has left a mark on each of these individuals—the island a sun around which they will forever orbit to some degree—and to read these unflinching stories is to feel the poignant truth of actual lives and actual struggles. A collection that is as important as it is engrossing."
—**Skip Horack**, author of *The Other Joseph*, *The Eden Hunter*, and *The Southern Cross*

"*Oye, What I'm Gonna Tell You* gives us an urgent glimpse into the lives of people yearning to fully understand their place in the world. Through these myriad voices, Milanés evokes a sense of the vital oral traditions that have shaped our community. These stories enrich and complicate an important, relevant conversation about what it means to exist on the hyphen— be it that of Cuban-American or any other truly American experience."—**Jennine Capó Crucet**, author of *How to Leave Hialeah* and *Make Your Home Among Strangers*

"To be of color in America is to know difference in a profound way. In *Oye, What I'm Gonna Tell You*, Cecilia Rodríguez Milanés writes a risky, remarkable, and necessary story collection. Milanés creates extraordinary characters each of whom is striking out for territory unknown, both geographically and personally. There is a resilience of spirit in her Cuban-American characters, who make a home that is a hybrid of two worlds. Fresh and evocative, this is the story collection you'll want to read this year."—**Nina McConigley**, author of *Cowboys and East Indians*, winner of the 2014 PEN Open Book Award

MORE PRAISE FOR *OYE WHAT I'M GONNA TELL YO*

"With *Oye What I'm Gonna Tell You*, spellbinding storyteller Cecilia Rodríguez Milanés delivers on that you-must-listen-up promise of her title, gifting readers with a pitch-perfect array of characters and voices that captivate, c

OYE
What I'm
Gonna
Tell You

OYE
What I'm
Gonna
Tell You

Stories

Cecilia Rodríguez Milanés

Brooklyn, New York

Printed in the United States of America
10 9 8 7 6 5 4 3 2 1

No part of this book may be used or reproduced in any manner
without written permission of the publisher. Please direct inquires
to:

Ig Publishing
392 Clinton Avenue
Brooklyn, NY 11238

ISBN: 978-1-63246-004-2

"The Law of Progress" first appeared online at *Guernica* and
republished in a slightly different version in the *Guernica* Annual
2014 volume. "Love and Punishment at the Clerk of the County
Courts Office" first appeared online at *Literary Mama* as was "Dr.
Cubanita" at *Kweli Journal.* "Other People's Homes" was first
published in *Seeds*, The Biannual Literary Journal of the Sisters of
Color. "What Remains of Max" was previously published in *The
Free Press* and "Barbie Doll" was first published *The Albany Review.*

*For familia, especially the cousins
y todos los que han llegado.*

CONTENTS

NIÑAS DE CASA

Getting ready for work at the dollar store, Celeste pulled a loose fitting khaki shirt over her dark blue pants to hide a small waist that gave some men the wrong idea about her. Like the day manager, a sweaty heavyset Americano who always snuck up behind her when she was stocking shelves or taking a quick bathroom break. "Oh, I was worried. I couldn't find you," he would say, brushing his soft body against her in the corridor between the back and the front of the store. She avoided his pale eyes as much as possible; they seemed to unclothe and dissect her at the same time.

She had had to get a job to help the family when her brother brought home his pregnant seventeen-year-old girlfriend. To Celeste, it was a tolerable job compared to the other intolerable "offer" to work in the hot, grease-covered kitchen of the burger place Papá had been at for years before he'd moved on to a real sit-down restaurant next to the mall. Enduring embarrassment and even discomfort at the dollar store was bearable because it was walking distance from her family's apartment and the hours were flexible enough that she could keep going to vo-tech school at night and complete her nurses' assistant course within a year.

She had arrived in this country from the island as an awkward, pimply preteen with her parents and older brother Camilo. He'd had a more difficult time adjusting to the U.S.

than she did; he left behind a big circle of friends and a novia while she only had one dear amiguita from school. At fifteen, Camilo was too old to fit in and he didn't seem to try too hard either, always getting suspended for fighting. But she, being the compliant girl that she was, respected her teachers and elders, dedicated hours to learning English and earned good grades from middle school on. She even went to catechism though she was the oldest girl to make her first holy communion among the more than 200 little children.

Celeste's naturally long nails fingered the gold cross and religious medals on her chain as she stood before the mirror remembering that day. "I'm so proud of you, mi niña; it's so good that you stuck with those classes," Mamá said, putting her sun-stained hands on her face before tightly embracing her. Celeste loved Mamá's smell and breathed deeply to take in the mariposa perfume made from Cuba's national flower. Papá had handed her an assortment of rainbow-colored carnations; he was wearing the ill-fitting suit the Catholic agency had given him in Miami years earlier. They were there all four together as a family. But soon they would be six.

She wondered if her almost-sister-in-law Kati wanted her to be godmother to the baby; they liked each other, were about the same age, had attended the same schools but had already had two very different lives. Kati had a rose tattoo above her left breast and was violently thrown out of her house after Camilo got her pregnant, and then she dropped out. Celeste wasn't against babies, she just wanted to do all things right, at the right time.

The last time Celeste went to church, she found herself at the altar, in a coffin, dressed in white for her funeral mass. The store manager had cornered her one too many times in the break room. The last time, he took and broke her, a good girl, una niña buena de casa. Choked to death by thick alien fingers, she was never to nurse or hold her new niece. Not even nineteen, she will always be eighteen in her senior photo with a blue crystal rosary hung around the frame and assorted santos' candles beneath. Some of the family's mighty grief was spent convincing Kati to name the baby after their niña. But Kati refused. Even so, they dedicated themselves to raising another good girl just like their Celeste.

For her mami and abuela, Magi was the sun and the stars. "Una muchacha buena, rebuena," abuela'd say to anyone in shouting distance, embarrassing the petite young woman with hazel eyes and a mass of black curls pulled up high on her head.

"Never, not once, did she bring me any problems to the house," her mami proudly proclaimed. "On the contrary, my Magi liked to help people."

It was true. Magi massaged her mami's sore feet from standing all day at the beauty parlor and she also always held onto abuela's arm when they walked together. Magi even watched her cousin's twin babies on weekends for free because she knew Irene was going crazy from missing so much school and was starting to get careless with them.

While mami and abuela would spend most of their limited telephone conversations sniveling about the tragedy and injustice of his imprisonment, Magi was the one who wrote her papi long letters to ease his time. They all lived convinced that their Magi was so good, so smart that she would know better, that she would steer clear of the disaster that was cute lil' Jova.

But his sob story and year in juvenile detention charmed the honor student right off her feet.

She wrote to her papi saying *I can change him.*

Papi understood the impulse; good girls always try changing bad boys.

Lil' Jova gave Magi some weed, showing her how to inhale, making silly faces she found irresistible, reminiscent of ones her papi made when she was little. Jova showed her a lot of things her papi should have warned her about, like when Jova convinced her to sell pills for him.

"Babe, I'm eighteen now. I can't get caught again, ma—no more juvy for me."

And she couldn't bear to lose him too.

Before long, Magi's AP classmates knew she was the one with the good stuff and lots of it. Jova said to pitch it as "better than their prescribed speed shit." Magi was blind in love and in trust; she couldn't see that Lil' Jova was not educable nor interested in reform. She especially couldn't see that he was making some bad deals.

"It was bad luck, such terrible, horrible luck that she was with that delinquent when the car was shot up," through tears, mami tells papi over and over again.

Abuela waits her turn. "Instantly gone, our niña," she'll say. "At least she didn't suffer, a mercy for sure."

Xiomara was no longer a girl but had always been a good one en casa. She had stayed on the relentlessly more oppressive island until the last parent died. Then she was an orphan, a woman without familial obligations—free of duty. The greatest risk she had ever taken was using all her little money to buy a space on the neighbor Rufino's unsteady boat—four days lost at sea while sun, wind or rain assaulted them, sometimes all at once, were well worth the price of a new life.

Once resettled and then settled, she charged forward trying marriage. Twice. She found it difficult for two grown people to get used to each other and it was especially challenging for Xiomara since she would have to adapt to the husbands' "real" families.

A failure at marriage, she tried living together too but the same problems surfaced. What commitments could she require of her first novio when he had so many obligations himself? Three children from three different mothers—all of them calling, texting, asking all the time for money for food, clothes, diapers or just a ride, just this time. "Sí, ya, ok," he'd say but it was never only one time.

Xiomara's second novio's children were grown, with children of their own and didn't want her at the family gatherings because it was the legitimate grandmother's place.

She resigned herself as not lucky in love and because she had no progeny, there were no uncomfortable attachments to the men. No reason for them to communicate with her even though she was a sweet, good woman.

After all of the drama of husbands and boyfriends, Xiomara came to the realization that she only needed her doggie, her painting (she discovered a talent!), her opera CDs and books on spirituality which kept her mind nourished. As a woman resigned to aloneness, it was her pleasure to help people, volunteering to spend time with elders twice a week—she liked listening to their stories, sometimes she offered her own. Everyone at the nursing home —viejitos and staff alike commented on her affectionate, caring manner. How could she suspect the young neighbor she called *un bebe?*

Xiomara didn't know that some monsters come with baby faces. He knocked on her door late one night.

"I'm sorry to bother you, Miss. I don't have my keys. Can I wait inside 'til my family gets home?"

It was raining heavily. The wind tried to shut the door but she was a good-hearted woman who had been brought up as a niña de casa, with some culture, a well-mannered, good person who he strangled almost to death—saved her to rape her all night.

But she finished the job the next day, taking all the pills she had in the house.

Roxana felt heart sick; that's what the aching, tight chest and cried out burning eyes had to be. And especially her brain hurt; she couldn't concentrate at school and ultimately brought home a mixed report card that her parents weren't happy with in the least.

What did they expect? A on top of A on top of A, all the way down the column, that's what they expected, she thought to herself. She had done it so many times before, her teachers talked to her about college, like it was a given, but now Roxana was thinking of other things besides getting good grades and making her family proud. It all started with the murder of Celeste, her co-worker at the dollar store.

Why hadn't Celeste said something about that asshole manager? Over and over Roxana asked herself this question on the way to, while at and after work. Before long, she messed up the register drawer count a couple of times and her hours were cut. Still she thought about the times they worked together. How they both rolled their eyes when the brute (Celeste didn't agree that he was bruto, just strange) inevitably called one of them into the back for some stupid thing or other. Roxana considered him slow and basically harmless, definitely not as mean as their woman manager who never smiled. Celeste worked mostly days so Roxana only saw her every other weekend when they were scheduled together. They weren't that close, but all of a sudden this person she knew, talked to and laughed with, was gone. She liked how Celeste used to paint her nails and thought her Miami accent was "super cute" though Celeste said she couldn't hear it herself. Roxana tried to remember a sign, any sign that would have led her to say something, but like Celeste, she was expected to not make a fuss. It was expected that a "pretty young thing" like her would attract unwanted attention. That was what the police officer said when he questioned Roxana about the manager, whose self-inflicted gunshot splattered blood over Celeste's still body and throughout the break room.

"Didn't he harass you too?" Roxana thought he was accusing her of something but she wasn't sure what.

It was so hard to go back to the store; her father said he understood and wondered if she shouldn't be working at night at all.

Lately Roxana had been fussing at home. Mamá attributed her talking back—under her breath, of course—to too much freedom. As if Roxana had time to be free—school all day, work at night and then cleaning up around the house after her spoiled brothers who never picked up a damn sock, shoe or shirt on their way out of the house for God-only-knows-where and until whatever fine hour they felt like. And neither one got criticized for bringing home a disappointing report card. Papá actually praised Rafa for standing up to the bully harassing Kiki even though they both got suspended for a week.

The grumbling got worse when her classmate Magi was shot. Roxana couldn't understand how such a smart girl could let herself get caught up with that known fool. Third period English with Ms. Brown was the A.P. class that Roxana had together with Magi— that and the same lunch schedule. Roxana remembered the essay Ms. Brown made Magi read aloud; it was about how she used to translate for her family all the time, even when she was really young. There were a couple of other kids in class who identified with that but Magi's essay was also funny because she described scenarios when she had no idea what was said and she'd make all sorts of crazy stuff up. It was clear that Magi was the best writer in class; maybe that's why she said she wanted to write a book. That's a book Roxana would have loved to have read.

Whether she was doing dishes or folding clothes, riding the bus or just walking through the chaotic hallways between classes, Roxana tried to sort out all the feelings reverberating in her head. Her parents always wanted to know where she was at all times, yet, Rafa and Kiki wouldn't even answer when Mamá made her call their cell phones when it is really late. Celeste's murder and Magi's, within weeks of each other, knocked something loose inside Roxana. Of course, there had been grief counselors brought to school; everyone who had classes with Magi had to listen, but these people didn't know her, know that she was popular even before Jova got to her. Everybody loved Magi though Roxana noticed afterwards that nobody was really that close to her. Except him. And wouldn't you know it, that fucker survived?

The last straw for Roxana was when she learned that her neighbor, that nice lady Xiomara was dead; her suicide note left horrible details. All Mamá could say was "La pobre, you should go to the mass for her, mija. I won't be able to get off work, but you should go." It wasn't even a special mass, only her name was read out, Xiomara Gómez Prado. Just like the mass when Celeste's name was added to the prayers of the faithful—her mother and grandmother bust out in tears and wailing so loud they had to be escorted out of the church, they were that wrecked.

After hearing Xiomara's full name out loud now, Roxana was struck by how little she knew about her too. She used to walk her small white dog around the block, always stopped to say hello to the neighbors sitting on porches or stoops. Roxana's mother once commented on the pretty flower-covered tote bag Xiomara carried, and within a week, she painted one for her. Roxana sat immobile through the rest of the service, progressively getting agitated while thinking hard about her recent dead, killed, she reasoned, because they were defenseless females. Why in the hell did Xiomara let that punk in her house, anyway? Roxana was sure it had something to do with being nice.

She had forgotten the words to the prayers and ignored the collection basket passed around her. Roxana wondered why her own mother had tried so hard to make her into a niña de casa. She even believed now that Mamá had, in fact, prepared her for harassment—"Put on lipstick before you go out!" "Smile and don't use foul language, that's for loose women," "Wear bright colors, nice young girls like you should always use colores alegres," along with the numerous reprimands about her bad posture, chipped, unpainted hands and sloppily brushed hair. It was always something, and not just her looks but everything; she had to be a well-liked, nice girl, all while earning good grades, helping in the house, and above all, being respectable.

When the young man seated in front of her turned around to share the sign of peace, Roxana stared wildly. She shook her head and wondered aloud, "Why peace when there is war?" Good girls like Magi, Celeste, and even la pobre Xiomara, were casualties, groomed by some bullshit about being nice. Roxana understood this and its significance for herself. She immediately wanted to yell. To stand at the ambo and preach would be even better, to tell all the niñas in church, at school and in the street to listen up, and know that the rules of la casa weren't made for their own good because they required unquestioned obedience. Putting up with so much shit (Roxana could already list a thousand stupid things) requires too much concentration.

Roxana bolted out of her seat and left the pew, muttering to herself; people looked at her contorted, grimaced face. She didn't care to be pretty anymore; she knew that sapped energy she could use to read between the lines of the niña script. Better to learn how to kick ass, she thought; better to fight with teeth and nails and to see clear-eyed into danger. To understand the power of a scream, of the "No" she did shout out as she pushed open the big glass doors with a force that made the priest pause abruptly and the congregation turn in disapproval. As Roxana rushed through the church narthex and stepped purposefully out into the street, worries about what others thought did not even cross her mind.

THE LAW OF PROGRESS

My mother's mother used to say that it took four generations to get the black out. I'm the fourth generation, so who I mate with will determine if our family racially advances or goes back. Atraso, that's what mami says whenever she sees light skinned people with black folks and their mixed, swirl babies. And get this, she swears it was a law in Cuba. For real. Abuela called it la ley de atavismo. You can't make shit like that up. If only she knew that I'm dating a Haitian dude. Not even fifteen fucking generations will get that black out!

Good thing abuela's dead; the shock of seeing her muñeca con ese negro tinto would kill her for sure. She's probably rolling in her grave all the way back to Cienfuegos where all her people are from. I could just hear her now: *We left everything so that you would never have to struggle and what do you do but go with un hatiano? Dios mío! You don't know what you're going to endure! Don't you know how you, how your children are going to suffer?*

Abuela was hardcore and never held back. There was this one time when I was ten and playing jacks out front with Shelly and Lisa, the sisters from across the street, their mom and dad were teachers for chrissake. So abuela's looking out the window and starts hollering: "Niña, ¿qué tú haces con esas negritas? Hazme el favor de entrar ahora mismo!"

"What she say?" Lisa was the smartest girl in fifth grade

and Shelly had already skipped a grade. I was so scared they'd understand I started yelling back and causing a ruckus.

"Abuela! ¿qué te pasa? I swear to God, porque tú dices eso? I can't believe this . . ."

"What'd she say? What the *hell* did she say," Shelly was poking me even though she was younger. "She'd better not be saying nothing 'bout us."

"Ya, Abuela, voy, I'm coming. I gotta go. Voy, Abuela."

The sisters were giving me the evil eye and I was breathing hard. I grabbed up the jacks and flew up the stairs without looking back. Abuela was still talking shit but thank God it was in Spanish.

I miss her but not her crazy-ass backwards thinking. For sure mami's not gonna be pleased about Vital; she is after all abuela's spawn. But Papi's harder to figure. Who knows what Papi's liable to do—just hope he doesn't put me out. We'll see.

My sister Neli, who's only fourteen months younger than me, laughed her ass off when I told her I was thinking of bringing Vital home. "Girl, have you lost your mind?" She advised me to keep him to myself. She can say shit like that because she's a lesbian so no man will ever "spoil" papi's little girl. Bitch didn't even get a hard time from the parents when she came out. Mami was all crying and shaking her head but she didn't cuss her out or disown her or nothing. And what came out of Papi's mouth just blew my mind (and made Neli run over and hug him tight). Something about how guajiros always say that a woman who goes with a woman first will never go with a man. Believe that shit?

Now she is the apple of their eye, always treating her tender, like she's so frail or something. But truth is, she's getting over on them. At least I think so because she quit school her senior year, saying she was so traumatized, pobrecita. Started working in a bike shop on the boulevard for her girlfriend who's older by twenty years (mami and papi sure as hell don't know that part) and Neli doesn't even pay rent or give money for food or nothing.

Me, I got my own car that I paid for (granted it's a piece a shit but it rolls) and I'm going to school days at Jersey State and work nights and weekends at Bonus Office Warehouse on route 441. I started giving my parents half my paycheck when papi was laid off. Mami says I shouldn't and that they'll pay me back when papi goes to full time again but I said no. I pay my cell, my school stuff, the car insurance, clothes, all the incidentals. I'm so glad to have my own room and not have to worry about doing laundry, cooking or buying groceries. I hate the thought of all that boring but necessary work. My goal in life is to have enough money to pay someone else to do that shit for me. I'm not even thinking marriage or kids. Just starting a business where I reap what I sow. That's something papi always put in my head from when I was little; hija, he'd say, in this country you can be your own boss. I don't have the language or the years so I have to work for someone else. Pero you, you can accomplish anything. Work hard and nothing can stop you, hear me?

It's not like Vital is the first black guy I ever dated. But I guess the others don't count because I never told my family. I knew it was more trouble than it would be worth and none of them were candidates for meeting the family anyway. Mami liked it when I brought home the pale-eyed polack or otherwise-nondescript unethnic americanos. Funny how blacks aren't considered americanos to them; as if to be American, you gotta be white.

And of course, we're not americanos either. Now that's what I call atraso.

I've waited five months. Two months before I even let Vital touch me though I wanted him to, really bad. It's not even that he's so fine; he's kinda skinny but has the most amazing smile. Maybe his teeth look so white because he is so freaking dark but even in the bright sunlight, his smile dazzles, and his face . . . oh, his face changes and it changes me, draws me in. Mami'd say that his face is llamativo; well, she might say it if she gave him half a chance.

Vital's old school, no tats or earrings; shit, his hair is even shaved down close to his beautifully formed head. No facial hair and no baggy clothes. And oh my god, he's Catholic! If he weren't so dark, I'm sure my family would love him. Love him like I wanna love him. It's gotta be love. Why else would I risk it all by bringing him home? He's so respectful of me, calls when he says he's gonna call, shows when he says he'll be there. Dude is a dreamboat. I called him that and he was like, what?

"Dreamboat. Don't you know what that means?" We had already had sex a couple of times and I was feeling high from skin and sweat and slick sweetness.

"What is this?" he blinked his sleepy, almond-shaped eyes and slid his hand over my cheek.

"It's like . . . ah . . . aw, hell, I don't know how to explain it. Someone who's like . . . perfect. The perfect guy."

He just grinned. He didn't tease me either but leaned over to plant a big ole wet one. Then he put my face in his hands and said something even I understood. "Je t'aime, mamacita." I had to laugh at that because of the time when I was walking toward him on campus, one of the hoodrats who thinks he's all that tried to get my attention, calling out, "Ay, mamacita, dame un pedacito." Which made me turn my head to laugh in his face which led to him saying "Bitch, why you do me like that?" Which led to Vital, who's not built but impressive because he's tall, getting up in the dude's face 'til he backed off. I guess if his boys were around it mighta turned out ugly. But right now I have this great guy, black like an azabache, telling me, he *loves me*, in freaking French, no less.

What I'm supposed to do? So I repeat but add my own twist. "Te quiero, papi chulo."

And we both bust out laughing.

So we go on doing our thing for a few more months, all good and soon enough it's Thanksgiving. Thanksfuckingiving. Shoulda thought that one through. After all, Neli doesn't bring her lady friend to the house. As far as they know, she's a virgin and will always be one.

I'd asked mami if I could bring a friend, un amigo, from school who doesn't have his family here and was alone for the holiday and as soon as I said that she gets all sentimental, "Ay, pobrecito. Sí, sí, invite him."

Vital was a little worried but I was all happy because mami had said yes. Of course, I said friend, not boyfriend.

"Your mother, she's ok with me going?" He raised his eyebrows and the skin on his usually serene forehead folded into three rolls.

"Yea, yea, she's cool. I said I was bringing a male friend."

"So, you didn't clarify that we were dating?"

"No, not yet. I think it's best to take it slow. Once they meet how wonderful you are, they'll accept you."

"Accept me for what?"

"Like accept you to be my boyfriend?" I was starting to get a little nervous and Vital was still frowning and had narrowed his eyes.

"I'm not sure this is a good idea."

"Naw, don't worry, it'll be all right. You're just a friend who goes to school with me and who's all alone for the holiday." And even as I said that it sounded like a stupid made up story like so many lies I had perpetrated on my parents: that I was sleeping over my best friend Ivette's the nights I was with Vital (or any of the other tipos I was getting with before him). Or going back to high school when I was ditching school and going to the city or just eating shit all day at the mall. Or that the smoke on my clothes was from all the workers in the warehouse where it was still legal (mami nailed me on that one when I left a crumpled pack in my hoodie pocket). Or any of the times when I didn't have to lie but felt like it because I just didn't want to tell them where I was going or what I was going to do, even when it was harmless. It all came to a head on Thanksgiving.

Mami's sister Julia and her family, all eight of them, always came because even though their house is bigger, we had the biggest table and enough chairs and plenty of parking on the side. Tiá and tió, tió's mother, their three young brats and their oldest Yalisa, who's Neli's age, with her baby (the baby daddy was MIA as soon as she got pregnant so he fit perfectly into the desgraciado role). No one could mention his name even though Yalisa named the baby after him so he will always and forever be Junior.

No one from Papi's side ever came. His family stayed in en el campo in Cuba; he was the only one who left the little town near the little city of Remedios in Las Villas province. It's not called that anymore; papi said that after the revolution Fidel divided up the island into a bunch of provinces that didn't make sense. Before Santa Clara was the province next to Las Villas but now his town is in Villa Clara. Once papi started talking about Castro and the stinking revolution, it was hard to shut him up. He accused his five brothers and sister of being communists for staying. Papi was the only one who had gone all the way to the capital and then gotten himself on a boat during el Mariel. And even though papi's a guajiro who loves his plants and nature and shit, he wasn't allowed to stay in Miami because there were too many of them. He and forty other unsponsored guys were bussed to Jersey where he and mami met in a factory. Thank God he didn't stay in Florida or we'd be hicks like my cousins in Hialeah. Talk about atraso.

One time we drove down there to see tío Saúl, mami's brother, and his family, staying with them for almost the whole summer. They wanted to check it out, to see about moving. I couldn't believe how a city in Florida which I thought was a jungle could look like a city in Jersey but without sidewalks or places to hang out except for a boring mall without any decent stores (Neli didn't really care about clothes but even as a twelve-year-old I could tell everything was already out of style). I didn't mind sharing a room with Neli and cousins Yeny and Alisa because we were older and cooler and told 'em all kinds of nonsense like where babies came from and why penises were sometimes flat and other times sticking up or that they spit out stuff that looked like Ivory dishwashing detergent. Nights were fun, nice and cold—there was a window AC we could control and froze every night to make up for the blazing days.

Hialeah was all we ever saw that summer and it was ugly,

hot, humid, full of mosquitos and enormous, I mean freakishly huge, fucking-flying roaches. Me and Neli begged our parents to please please please never ever ever even consider moving there. I'm sure Papi was sad he wouldn't get to cultivate his mamey or mango or aguacate or whatever but luckily for us it didn't happen. Me and Neli were ecstatic about the "news" they sat us down to hear.

"Niñas," Papi did the talking for both of them. Our parents faced us as we sat in the backseat of our car, away from the relatives including abuela—it was the only place of privacy.

"Your mami and I have been really trying hard to make it work here," he said then bit his thick lower lip. Neli was banging her knees together real fast so I pinched her to stop.

"I wanted us to move here, to la Florida but there aren't any good jobs and without jobs, we can't take the chance." He looked at mami to see if she wanted to add something.

"And besides that, your papi and I wanted to buy a house," she smiled out of one side of her mouth. "Abuela has a little money to help us but she doesn't want to stay here."

I was surprised to hear that because abuela was always talking about how much she missed her son and the twins but, hell, she was on our side, for once.

"We know you girls didn't want to move but you're still young and you would have adjusted quickly. New Jersey is all you know; it would have been an adventure pero," he shook his head and massaged his neck, "it's just not the right time."

Right time? That made me keep up my guard so that at the end of every school year, I'd listen carefully to them talk about summer to catch wind of any plans on heading south but it never happened. Thank God, the saints and all the angels, amen.

Thanksgiving dinner at my house was a production because a regular everyday dinner was rice, beans, and some kind of meat—picadillo, thin steaks, chicken and every once in a while we'd have fish because abuela liked fish. Neli was charged with setting the table and I made the salad. Papi always brought home a loaf of day-old Italian bread—that was mami's dessert. Pretty simple meals. But Thanksgiving mami made a big American roasted turkey and also turkey fricasé because papi thought turkey was too dry. I asked her to make stuffing like I saw on TV but she didn't know what it was so I showed her the box in the store and then we always had it. Gravy, two kinds of cranberry, American yams and Cuban boniato, store bought pumpkin and apple pies. Instead of our typical rice and beans, tía Julia always brought her famous moros y cristianos—black beans cooked with white rice. Tía had a running joke about how the whites, the cristianos, liked the Africans, the moors, a little too much and we'd all laugh. But not tonight. And that was the beginning of the end of our happy thanksgiving dinner.

There was a racket, like always because that's how we are and any other day I wouldn't have noticed but today it seemed like everyone was amplified and I thought I shoulda warned Vital, who, of course, arrived right on time and wearing a nice dress shirt and jacket; he looked better than the rest of us put together. I made sure I was near the door so I could be the one to get it when he rang the bell.

"Hi," I said and looked back to see if anyone had followed me down the hall.

"Happy Thanksgiving," he said and gave me a bunch of orange, burgundy and yellow flowers and had another bunch left.

His dazzling smile steadied me as he crossed over the threshold into Casa de Locos.

"Everyone's here." I rubbed his arm and motioned for him to follow me. "Don't worry, we talk loud but it's fast so if you don't understand, give me a sign."

Vital lifted two fingers and I punched his shoulder and then we were inside the front room set up with the big table.

"Oye familia, this is my friend, Vital." It was just a split second pause but long enough for me to know. He said hello but it was real low and I think only me and Neli, who was sitting at the end of the table, heard.

Mami walked over to him first. He handed her the other flowers, even bigger than my bunch, smiling that smile and she smiled back then lowered her head in a weird bow. "Oh, thank you."

"Vital speaks French and Spanish," I rushed in before anyone said anything else. I wanted them to know that he'd understand if they started talking shit.

"Ah, that's good, qué bueno," Mami's eyebrows lifted.

Papi stood and reached out to shake Vital's hand. "Hello, hello," Papi's big hand covered Vital's, shaking hard.

"Buenas noches, señor," Vital kept flashing the smile, papi kept shaking his hand. "Gracias por la invitación."

Tía mumbled to tío something in Spanish about who invited him. Mami turned and gave her the don't-go-there look.

"Please, please, come and sit down." Papi steered him toward the other end of the table but Neli jumped up.

"Oh, no, come sit here next to me, I'm her sister, the younger, smarter one."

I didn't need any foolishness, especially not now. "Very funny, Neli, but he's going to sit next to me. I saved him a seat between me and mom."

"I don't want these beautiful flowers to dry up. Excuse me." Mami seemed in a hurry to get to the kitchen and I felt like going after her but my feet were stuck so I put my flowers on the back of the couch. "Go on then, go sit with your guest." And she took the flowers to the kitchen.

I shot her a confused look as she passed me.

Vital was pulling a chair out for me and the rest of the family was looking so I forced one foot in front of the other and made it to my place.

Tío reached over to shake Vital's hand, "Hello, I'm Joaquin," he motioned to his left, "my wife Julia, her aunt," and then motioned to his right, "my mother Lupe." Both of them nodded and weakly lifted a hand. "Those little animals are our kids," tío always called Brian, Quique and Carlitos his animalitos and they lived up to it. Then he stood to introduce his blameless princess, "Yalisa, and my nietecito, Junior." He lifted his hands and the baby reached out his fat arms.

"Ay, qué divino," Lupe said while tía cooed. I thought maybe the baby would keep them entertained with his gurgling and rapid-fire raspberries. Neli was already sitting and mami easing into her chair with papi at the head of the table.

Then Vital said, "What a beautiful baby! Where is the father?"

Neli stifled a laugh and I gasped. Tía turned toward tío and mumbled for him to walk the baby, just go. Yalisa bit her lip, the animalitos giggled and Lupe said, "Ay, Dios mío."

"He's gone, dead," Tía's angry frown confused Vital. I leaned over and whispered to the floor that he left my cousin.

"So, so sorry, lo siento," he tried to fix it but it was too late.

It was the longest, most miserable, most god-awful night. Nobody cracked jokes like we usually did, making fun of papi's fricasé and all the carbs and the lonely exquisite salad I made that nobody ever touched. We ate fast but without audibly savoring the meal; I missed papi's ooohing and ahhing over every single thing. Nobody asked Vital anything about Haiti or his family or what he was studying, or if he liked the food. Nothing. He was the black elephant in the room and I was the big pile of elephant shit. We usually ignored the bickering little kids but tonight the adults took turns yelling at them. And every time Vital spoke in Spanish it made them all even more uncomfortable. So tía's moros were passed around without comment and tío put Junior into the playpen but never returned to the table, not even when we said thanks to god for the food.

When it was time for dessert, Vital stood to help pick up the plates. "Por favor, quiero ayudar."

"No, no, please. Don't!" Mami was a little too insistent. I bit the inside of my cheek and brushed away a hot tear that popped out. Neli took the plates from the end of the table and I took the ones from the front. Even Yalisa stood and gathered up the forks and knives.

"You are a guest, you sit," Papi said, pointing at Vital.

By now I was pretty sure everyone had figured Vital was more than my friend. By now his smile had lost like ninety percent of its wattage and I'm saying a prayer that we get out this without any more damage.

Brian, Quique and Carlitos were banging their now empty fists on the table and asking for pie, pie, pie. From out of nowhere, tío appeared and slapped two of them at a time in the back of the head causing them to ricochet and then again to get the other one, and the unlucky one twice. The youngest one started balling and tía reprimanded the kids and tío while Lupe tried to calm them all. Yalisa rolled her eyes and said, "Here we go." This set tío off again and he laid into her.

"What are you complaining about?" Yalisa seemed genuinely surprised to see how annoyed he was then shocked when he lunged toward her and shook her shoulder. "Go take care of your son. He's your responsibility."

No one made a sound until mami came back from the kitchen with two pies. She surveyed the room, placed the pies in front of papi and asked how many wanted café and how many wanted coffee.

I'm responsible for the coffee so I got to work while mami violently packed the espresso down into the stainless steel basket of the Italian coffee pot. My tongue felt like sandpaper, my head a bowling ball and I could have kicked myself for thinking this all would have worked out.

Mami's giving me the silent treatment; abuela would have been cursing me, my Haitian and my mulato nappy-headed brood by now and I almost wished mami would say something she's twisting the lid so hard the veins in her neck ripple. I see no way out. No way to get Vital in. Nothing but hardship and I ask myself, why in the hell would this, us, work when all the evidence pointed to the disaster it became? I felt myself rehearsing the lie I'd perpetrate on him later. How we're too different and that I planned on moving to the city with Ivette, that I was transferring to CUNY. How much I would miss his dazzling smile. How he's too good for me. Later, I'll cry when he wants to soothe me to make it better.

ENOUGH OF ANYTHING

Alma grew up around whores and homosexuals. Because her mother was dead, she, along with her younger brother, Ricardo, lived in a boarding house run by their great aunt Lázara in a poor barrio in the east of Havana. Lala—as Lázara was known to all—was less indiscriminate than she was disinterested in the quality of the roomers who lived in the four single room apartments on the second floor, furnished with beds, hot plates and a shared toilet. Alma and Ricardo lived downstairs with tía Lala. They had three rooms—a big bedroom they all shared, a rarely-used sitting room, and a long, narrow kitchen with a back door leading to the toilet and a small yard.

In the front of the house was a half-enclosed balcony facing the street. Here, Lala spent her days smoking puros and drinking café she warmed on an ancient burner that worked better than the new ones the roomers had. From her perch, she kept track of the comings and goings of the tenants. Lala genuinely liked her tenants, as long as they kept out of trouble and paid their rent, that is. The longest staying roomer was Rosalinda, who Lala called "la pobre Rosalinda who is neither pretty nor smells like a rose" but never to her face.

Alma liked it when the roomers washed up and came downstairs with their wet hair still grooved with wide comb marks, shirts or shifts clinging to their bodies and always sweetly crisp-smelling. Sometimes, Rosalinda would give her three pennies to braid her long black hair in a neat plait that almost reached her tailbone. On Fridays, Marco, the most recent roomer whose blond hair was always perfectly coifed, sent Alma to the bodega for rolling papers and let her keep the whole five cents change; errands were a way tenants could tip the children and show Lala their appreciation. Lala permitted the roomers' affection toward the siblings because she was stingy with hers. She didn't like anyone touching her, though on occasion she allowed Alma to rub her plump little feet and sausage-like toes.

Sometimes one or two of the roomers would come downstairs to gossip, sitting or standing on the steps next to the balcony. They would call their landlord Doña Lala and tell dirty jokes or stories that Alma and her brother were warned by their aunt never to repeat at school. By the time she was nine years old, Alma understood all the components of sex, though she couldn't fathom how people could enjoy such acts, especially the kind requiring the unusual use of one's hindquarters. This knowledge gained Alma a measure of popularity at school when it was evident that no one else knew as much as she did. Even the older girls who had boyfriends named her la profesora of sexual studies.

"Oye, niña, what have you learned from your scandalous neighbors recently?" Three upper grade girls formed a circle around her.

Alma smiled broadly and, pointing to each girl at a time, said, "That your father likes to take it up the ass. That your father likes to put it there. And that your father likes to watch."

The girls erupted in howling laughter and curses.

"You shameless . . ."

"You sucia . . ."

"Hija de puta!" That was the one that stopped Alma in her tracks. Everyone knew where the line was. Her mother was not a whore. She was dead.

"I'm so sorry, I'm sorry." Micaela's hand shot up to her red painted lips as she stepped away. "I didn't mean it." The girl's friends moved to push her further back. They nodded to Alma, signaling that they would attend to Micaela's transgression, who continued apologizing even after Alma was out of earshot.

Alma and Riqui (a nickname her brother gave himself after eschewing the perennial Ricardito) attended a local public school in one of the suburbs of Havana with a mix of mid and lower working class folks. While they had the same full lips and wispy dark hair, they did not look like siblings, and the lighter-skinned Riqui liked to point out that he was the more guapo. Alma secretly agreed while protesting that his shapely legs were "such a waste on a boy."

Their aunt praised their "equal beauty" and made sure their uniforms were clean and starched stiff, always checked their head for lice, and fed them sufficiently, including a weekly swill of cod liver oil. Lala never let them walk around barefoot, declaring loudly she would not tolerate "worm-infested brats in her house" and forbade pets for the same reason. Alma could not conceive of how worms could get inside her body from her feet or a puppy, but she was an obedient girl who never questioned her aunt's authority. Riqui, a contrary boy famous for his on-call farts, wasn't ever spanked, only mildly scolded.

Their Mamá had been tía Lala's and tía Orfa's beloved and beautiful only grandniece Gladys. Tía Lala and tía Orfa used to live upstairs before there were any boarders and before Mamá was abandoned by her own mother. Alma knew only two things about her grandmother, who Lala derisively called "la estrella": that she worked in a casino and would wake them all up in the middle of the night so they could eat the food she'd brought home while it was still warm; and that she ran away with an americano to el norte to make movies. As for tía Orfa (who died of being old), Alma remembered very little, only that she had a broad dark stain that covered her right eye and cheek, like she had splashed that part of her face with reddish brown paint. Alma was still an only child when Orfa died, but old enough to fear kissing the birthmark. And Mamá, well, she remembered some things but more often she felt her as a persistent, sad ghost pressing on her absurdly flat chest.

Lala had helped tía Orfa, a respected yerbera, with Alma's birth, a five pound runt of a baby, but by the time the nine-pound beast Riqui was kicking his way out of Mamá, Lala was alone. She knew some herbs could ease the labor, but concentrated hours massaging Mamá's belly for the baby to turn around. After much struggle and screaming, Lala successfully helped Mamá bring Riqui to light but, what with all the difficulty of the labor and the size of the purple baby boy whose piercing cries could summon the dead, she forgot everything else that had to be done after cutting the umbilical cord so that some of the placenta stayed inside and there was a fatal infection.

In their bedroom was a big photo of Mamá in a tin cut frame next to an even bigger one of Our Lady of Regla. Lala made them pray to both every night, even though Riqui usually fell asleep before the second Hail Mary and Lala was snoring by the first Our Father. The blessed mother of the oceans' face smiled serenely in her blue gown, hands out at her sides, light rays shining all around, the sea sparkling behind her. She looked like a loving mother who would enfold you and grant any little thing you asked for, if what you wanted was pure.

Her mother's portrait lit by candles was a stark contrast. Alma would study her face; she had the same delicate curls and almond eyes but couldn't tell from the black and white photo what color they were. There seemed to be a melancholic expression at the corners of her closed mouth, and Alma wondered whether she knew she was going to die so young. Alma couldn't help blaming Riqui a little, though mostly she was jealous of the tenderness with which tía Lala occasionally treated him. But then again, Riqui couldn't remember what it was to smell Mamá's sweet neck or feel her soft fingertips circling her back as Alma did when they had nestled together every night.

Their father was even more of a ghost, an itinerant brush salesman who visited occasionally, then never returned, not even once to see his motherless baby boy; the only thing he left them was his last name, Delgado, which Lala regularly cursed. Alma couldn't remember what he looked like and there were no photos of him anywhere, though given Lala's influence she imagined him with horns and a forked tongue.

"Lala, why didn't you have children?" Alma asked one day after her best friend Loly started menstruating, claiming that she was now capable of bearing children, something Alma seriously doubted since her breasts were even flatter than hers. Alma was fifteen but hadn't yet started and probably wouldn't for a long time because she was so skinny. Jorgina, one of her classmates, thought she was being instructive when she showed a clutch of girls in the bathroom what the little towels looked like. Alma had already seen some used ones Rosalinda or Consuelo had discarded on the trash heap in the yard before Lala told them to be more discreet after Riqui brought one to the front porch to inspect.

"Pelucita, hija, el señor blessed me with the burden of raising my sainted niece and then her children," she said, then gestured for the girl's hand. "You will have your own children someday but not for a long . . ." She stopped short, biting her lip till teeth marks showed and Alma wondered if a burden could also be a blessing.

In tenth grade, Alma fell in love with Eduardo Domínguez, a poor classmate from around the way who knew how to do many of the acts Alma only knew how to describe, even some requiring the unusual use of one's hindquarters.

"Pelucita, meet me at the midday break," Eduardo whispered from behind her as they switched classes one morning. A chill shot down her spine as she nodded. His large-lidded eyes were wider today, she noticed. She bit her lip in anticipation of his fondling and it was difficult to sit still in the last class of the morning.

Alma found him near the walking ficus trees; he liked to pretend he was in jail behind the vines that had fastened to the ground. His crooked smile looked especially handsome to her; Loly didn't think he was, pointing to the missing canine and bowed legs but these things endeared him all the more to Alma.

"Mi amor," he reached to pull her behind the widest trunk, his big hands already moving over her.

"We only have a few minutes," Alma's smile tilted up just as her shoulder did.

"I know, I know. But we'll leave the loving for later." He kissed her forehead. "I have something to propose to you."

Alma's thin eyebrows arched.

"Here, let's sit down. Let me tell you what I have been thinking about." Eduardo's face was seized by excitement. "Querida, what would you say if I asked to you go with me to Oriente? Wait!" He held his hand up before Alma could interject. "I want us to be together all the time. It's impossible for me to concentrate on school when all I think about is being with you, holding you, playing with you until you scream with pleasure."

Alma had surprised herself with the first yelp that had escaped her lips when his suckled her. It was now his goal to elicit all matter of cries from her during their encounters. She bit her lip and let him continue.

"We could leave this place and become free! New people!"

Was it possible to become a new person in a new place, she wondered?

"No one to tell us what to do. I could work for us, for you! I'll do anything, cut caña, shine shoes even if I have to but it won't be like that. I promise, mi vida. It will be wonderful, an adventure. Imagine it, Alma mia!" He explained how they would make their escape, hopping aboard the westbound freight train that left before dawn from the yards nearby, riding in front of the sun and towards their destiny. He told her about the famous days-long carnavales that wound through the streets of Santiago de Cuba. He pointed out that the most important musicians came from that end of the island. She mentioned money; he said he had some, not a lot but enough. She asked when and he said, "Whenever you are ready."

"My love, with you, always but . . . give me a few days to earn some more pennies to add to yours." She kissed his hands that firmly grasped hers.

"As you say."

They parted and didn't even exchange glances in their only class together. Alma's blood raced and she felt warmth throughout her limbs while her heart thumped steadily with the promise of a different life.

Alma had every intention of dropping out of school. She could happily see herself running off with Eduardo to Santiago where, he reminded her, the music and dancing was the best on the island. However, a frantic Loly told on her to all the teachers. Señorita Álvarez, one of the more concerned ones, unafraid of their dicey neighborhood, went to talk to Lala, who started cursing as soon as she saw the teacher coming up the street.

She called Alma out to the porch. "What is the meaning of this, niña?" she said through teeth locked on a cigar butt.

"I don't know, tía Lala," Alma had already hidden a little piece of cloth in the back of the armoire, wrapping her only blouse and skirt without faded patches or stains, her sandals, some barrettes and Mamá's comb.

"If you have done anything!" Lala raised her hand high, threatening the violence Alma had personally never experienced but had witnessed, having seen tía thrash half-dressed men who mistreated her roomers going down the stairs out into the street where everyone taunted the fleeing "degenerates." Shouts of "maricón" or "animal" would follow the singled-out man until he turned the corner and was out of the neighbors' view.

Lala hiked up her prodigious breasts and slowly made her way down the stairs to the street. She had no intention of letting the teacher in the house without a good reason.

"What is it that you want?"

"Buenas tardes, señora. I come about the girl. Is it possible to speak inside?"

Lala wagged her finger from side to side, then gestured for Alma, already shaking with hot tears slipping down her cheeks, to go inside. Alms considered grabbing her bundle and running out through the rear of the house, though that would require climbing over the fence into the mechanic's yard where a big German Shepard growled menacingly whenever anyone was near. Instead, she stood behind the door frame to hear what she could as Lala would never kill her but the hulking black and gray demon dog surely would. The teacher told Lala everything.

After she left, Lala came into the hot, narrow kitchen where Alma was pretending to stir the frijoles. She approached without a word and slapped Alma across the face. That afternoon, Eduardo's family pulled him out of school and sent him to work on his abuelo's finca in Las Villas. Alma made a deal with the Virgin; if the sainted mother would see to it that she'd be reunited with Eduardo, she promised to say seven extra Hail Marys every night and name her first daughter Reglita, dedicating her to Yemayá.

To bring in some extra money, Alma took to mending things for the roomers. Sometimes, while she was fixing something or sewing on a button, Lala would tell her stories from the past.

"Can you even imagine how poor we were when all the men died?" Tía's grandfather, father and uncles, including Mamá's father, had all died in the last revolution, when Cuba was

liberated from España. "Your aunt Orfa was a lot older than me
. . . She and I were little girls and our mamá was alone so she
asked all three sisters-in-law to come stay here. Our house was
brand new then, the only one on this hill," Lala gestured to the
left, to the right, then left again. "There was nothing here, can
you imagine it? Abuelo had come to live here after Abuelita
Victorina died. Papá provided, thanks to God and our virgencita
de Regla." Alma knew that he had worked at the port, though
she wasn't sure exactly what he did but that it was a job with
enough income for a house full of females after the war, when
there wasn't anyone else to provide enough of anything.

"Porbrecita Mima, she tried her best to feed us all but after
the men were dead and buried, the sisters-in-law returned to
their own families. We never heard from them up to this day."
Lala didn't dwell on the betrayal her mother felt in favor of
drawing out the description of their poverty. "Do you know
what piltrafa is?" Lala widened her bloodshot eyes as she asked.

"I can't remember, tía." Alma said, feigning ignorance,
hoping for new details. "Something like a soup?"

"Ha! If only it were even half of a soup like you know today."
Lala scratched her double chin. "As much as Mima insisted it
was soup, I never thought it was because I remembered the
tremendous soups she used to make before with lots of meat
chunks in it and special thin noodles. For the piltrafa, Mima
would walk all the way to the mercado over by the big traffic
circle, where la Virgen of the Way's statue sits, us girls walking
alongside her. Niña, you know how far that is, right?"

Alma nodded in silence, her eyes focused on a button hole
she was meticulously repairing.

"Mima would go to the meat market twice a week. Ay, Orfa

and I hated the smell and all the flies but there wasn't a living soul who Mima trusted with 'confianza' to watch us, especially the roomers she had started to take in. Why, they looked as poor as we were! So off we went every few days—with no icebox, what more could you expect? Mima would ask the butcher for the scraps left over from the beef cuts. Only a few people could afford beefsteak then, even worse than now. Do you know what I'm talking about, niña?"

Alma wasn't sure if she meant the scraps or the people who brought steak. Before she could ask, Lala continued.

"The white strips of tendon and muscle. That's piltrafa and it was usually for the rich people's dogs or poor people like us. Mima would get the little piece of pork she could afford and there was one butcher who knew she was a widow alone with two niñitas so he'd save her some scraps that still had a little meat for her. Do you believe it?"

Alma didn't have to answer because Lala had closed her eyes, signaling the end of the storytelling. Alma could fill in the rest, how the scraps would be put into a big pot of boiling water to get the flavor of meat so that any viands they had would taste more than the tasteless, starchy tubers they were; how that was what sustained them. That and their prayers to Our Lady, of course.

Her little mending jobs gave Alma some extra money to buy discounted material to sew herself a new dress from time to time. No longer flat-chested, her brown nipples were the yokes of what Lala called "two fried eggs." Eduardo would have liked to have tasted these, Alma thought, remembering the latest letter he'd sent. Alma had started receiving the crumpled letters that his older sister Olga handed to her in grammar class at the Escuela Superior.

That first letter began with "If this letter reaches you, mi querida, know that I love you and only want to be with you day and night, especially in the night." This line made Alma tremble in a way only Eduardo's touch had previously accomplished. He told her about the countryside near Camajuaní, how there were royal palms everywhere, how rich the soil and green the plants were. He said that there were so many birds he never knew existed and they sang songs every morning and even in the night that made his head spin but that nothing, darling Alma, was "as beautiful as the look you give just before a kiss."

His abuelo, he wrote, like most guarijos, left the bohio early each day for the cane fields and returned after dusk. He didn't want this for his grandson, so he had made a plot of tobacco Eduardo's responsibility. In large loopy script, Eduardo described how much trouble it took to get the seedlings to grow into long luscious leaves ready for the drying shed. He said the leaves smelled sweet and that they were just as good as those grown in Pinar del Río where everyone said most of the island's best tabaco was cultivated. His abuelo rolled his own cigars and sold the rest of the crop for cheap to neighbors or friends in the nearby pueblos like Taguayabón and as far as the small city of Remedios where he learned that they had the best Christmas carnavales. With pride, Eduardo told Alma that he got to keep a percentage of the tobacco profits and that he was saving money to come get her.

Alma considered a sacrifice to Yemayá, in order to prove her dedication to Eduardo. A whole watermelon, the goddess' favorite fruit, to pray over and drop into the high tide at the malecón. She took to carrying seven copper coins in her pocket, using them as a rosary for Our Lady, passing each from pocket to pocket once the Hail Mary was completed.

One day, tía Lala said she needed to speak with her on a serious matter and led her into the sitting room. It felt strange to Alma being there because she couldn't remember the last time they'd used the room.

Lala arranged her large loose hips in a finely carved armchair she said had been her grandmother's and asked loudly why Alma's hand in marriage hadn't been promised by now.

"Hurry up and find a man, Pelucita. But a good, honorable man. I don't want any no-count machos around here, especially the kinds that would have you run away from her family. A decent, hardworking man is what I want for you, Pelucita."

Alma wondered if tía would ever give Eduardo the chance to prove himself. She looked above and beyond Lala's agitated head to the framed saints in the bedroom.

"First thing I will do is send everyone . . ." this she said more quietly as she pointed upstairs, "packing! Solavaya todo el mundo! You and your husband would have the whole upstairs so you could make lots of children to fill those rooms." She laughed a little, then looked away. "You know, niña, I'm not getting any younger."

Alma saw the vision Lala had for her: selfless caretaker cleaning up after her aged great aunt and attending to the anticipated brood for the rest of her life, nothing but the same, cruel routine of old lady sicknesses or baby diarrhea, never seeing anything beyond the outskirts of Havana. (Lala wasn't expecting Ricardo to take care of her; he'd joined the navy as soon as he could and was now sending home giddy postcards from New Orleans or Alabama and recently Key West where he was stuck for months awaiting his ship's repair but never once, ever, did he send any money.) Alma's throat constricted and her chest followed suit. It was as if her blood had slowed to molasses.

As Alma began her last year of high school, Eduardo's letters started to arrive less frequently. In the early days of their separation, Olga would hand Alma a folded envelope every week. Alma would thank her, then unseal the envelope and read the letter through quickly, right on the spot. Then she would read it again, memorizing each flourish and dot on the thin paper. Once she'd committed it to memory, she ripped the paper into shreds and deposited allotments of the little pieces throughout the school, in each classroom's wastebasket.

Now, it was only on rare occasions that Olga gave her a letter. Alma wasn't even sure Eduardo got her letters, since his never remarked on her questions or the latest gossip. Eventually, Alma stopped writing back.

One afternoon, Olga approached Alma in the school courtyard. "Oye, I'm sorry to tell you this, chica, but my brother has gone to el norte with our mother's brother."

Alma gasped.

"Tío Andrés has the opportunity of work in a factory."

Alma couldn't speak. Olga neared, touching her shoulder. "I wouldn't wait for him anymore," she said, softly patting Alma's back before walking away.

For the last two and a half years, she had been dismissing would-be suitors, even though she was sure tía Lala would have liked her to bring any one of them home since they were nothing like her beloved. She had been secretly saving one peso a month for their getaway. She wondered what she would do with her nest egg now.

A few weeks later, Olga handed her one final letter. It described the teeming, wonderful city of New York, and the less so New Jersey (he put "nueva yor" and "nu yersi" in parentheses so she'd know how to properly pronounce them). There was no mention of love or sex, not even one word or a damned syllable of yearning. Her disappointment was now tempered by her anger. She had watched as her classmates paired off, ready to start their adult lives. Her heart had been set on Eduardo for too many years, forbidding anyone else's entry. A little knot of despair made its debut and lodged itself squarely in her throat.

"So, my friend, who is coming to the graduation reception with you?" Loly asked one afternoon near the end of the school year as they walked toward the bus stop. The upper school in their district had burned down, displacing students entering the last two grades, and Alma and her classmates had been sent to school in Havana proper, a real city, not a barrio. It was like a miracle for Alma and Loly, who had cemented their friendship while exploring the Paris of the Caribbean. On Fridays after school they went to the cinema in el Vedado; if the girls were disturbed by the newsreels full of war, they were quickly soothed by the peculiar American versions of love and life towering over them in Technicolor. On Sundays after church in the old cathedral, they'd stroll around the plaza and the surrounding cobblestoned streets, sharing guanábana shakes. For a five-cent bus ride, they snuck away to the university district every chance they got. But today, a Tuesday, they were headed back to the eastern suburbs.

"My God, Loly, don't you have anything else to worry about?" Alma answered. She had deliberately avoided thinking about her future. "Your hair, maybe? Or your cross-eyed old man boyfriend?" Alma shoved her a little harder than she meant to; she hadn't revealed the contents of Eduardo's final letter.

"Ay, enough! He is not my boyfriend," Loly laughed. "He is just a friend of the family with money and the desire to marry."

"Oye, niña, can you imagine the drooping skin on that viejo's culo? His testicles probably drag behind him when he's not wearing calzoncillos." They both laughed so hard they had to wipe their eyes.

As they reached the bus stop, they saw that their bus was gearing up to depart. They shouted after the unfamiliar driver, who refused to open the door as he pulled away.

"Desgraciado!" Alma yelled, then motioned toward a nearby bench in the shade of some fragrant old mango trees lining the small plaza. "I wonder where our Juanito is today. He would never have left us like that."

Loly settled herself then looked Alma in the eye. "So, listen to what I'm going to tell you. A secret, my friend and you must swear to God almighty and all the virgins and saints that you will not say anything to anyone or especially to my father," she said, holding Alma's shoulders.

"Have mercy! Blanca Dolores Iriarte Romero, what in the world have you done?" Alma was surprised at her prim and proper friend's spellbound expression; she'd never seen it before, and wondered what benign mischief she might be plotting.

"Nothing. It's what I'm *going* to do."

Alma cocked her head. "Loly, by God, spill it."

"I am going to el norte," Loly's inflection ended in a little squeal.

"What are you saying?"

"Yes, querida Pelucita, I am going to leave this bloody island and its backwards old-fashioned ways!"

Alma could hardly catch her breath as Loly divulged her intricate plan: by ship to Miami, bus to New Jersey—not New York, which was already overrun by immigrants—room at a Galician señora's boarding house in Bayonne where she'd work in a lace factory Fulana told her about and then, finally she would find a Cary Grant lookalike. Alma couldn't believe this was all coming from a girl she'd always considered so conservative, the kind that foolishly believed in the value of her virginity.

"I refuse to marry that viejo shit-pants. Just because Papá is twenty years older than mami doesn't mean I have to make the same mistake." Loly stopped, considering how she'd described her parents' marriage to a friend without parents. "I mean, I know that's how it was done in the past but, coño, that's history." She took a deep breath and let out a deeper sigh that she seemed to have been holding a while. "America is modern and I am a modern woman so that's where I belong! I'm suffocating, Alma; my mother says that this is the best time of my life. That after marriage, a woman is completely dedicated to her house, her children and serving her husband." Loly sighed again. "That is the best time? No jodes! We have hardly begun to live! Right, chica?"

"Oh, yes, of course. We will never be young again." Alma's answer sounded pro forma but it didn't slow her friend down a bit.

"Yes, yes, we are young and beautiful," Loly said, laughing.

"And besides, who doesn't want to marry a tall, handsome American buck like that Clark Gable, Tyrone Power or, o el guapo Cary Grant? Don't you?"

Alma imagined Eduardo in a factory in New Jersey, before her thoughts turned to the most famous American city of New York. It had to be wonderful in real life because the movies made it out to be larger and more real than life. She was trying to imagine herself there, dressed in American clothes, a stylish hat, delicate gloves and heels to make her tall like the Americanas, walking purposefully, confidently into possibility.

"Don't you?" Loly repeated.

"Don't I what?"

"Don't you want to meet an Americano with sky blue eyes and so tall you have to get on tippy toes to kiss him?" Loly was swooning in her fantasy.

"Loly, how much is the passage? To Miami?"

"What?"

"How much does it cost to get to Miami? And then to el norte?"

"What the devil are you talking about? Alma, of my life, are you . . .?" She searched Alma's rapidly blinking eyes. "Tell me, please." Now Alma was the one with the enthralled expression at the thought of freedom. She calmed herself in order to speak slowly but convincingly, "Oh, for god's sake, Loly, don't be ridiculous." She smirked and continued. "I was just thinking about where in the world you would get that kind of money, but then I remembered you sold your little ass on the avenue!"

"Alma!" Loly lightly punched her arm and stomach several times as they both collapsed in a fit of laugher.

Traffic had clogged the avenue, so they decided to walk

home. They walked and talked all the way to the edge of Alma's barrio where Loly kissed her before turning back toward her own.

"I'm leaving Thursday, after our domestic economy class."

"But the graduation?"

"I have to. I can't bear to see that viejo again. I overhead him saying to Papá that he was planning to present me with his long dead mother's ring. Ay, the thought disgusts me!"

Alma sighed as she kicked at the curb. "I will miss you, cabrona." Despite the genuine sadness that had overcome her, Alma was already adding up figures in her head.

After Loly left, her old father was desperate enough to come to Alma's neighborhood one day in search of information about his daughter.

"Niña! There is someone here to talk to you," Lala called excitedly from the balcony. Alma hadn't detected an accusatory tone; after all, she hadn't done anything. Yet.

"Señor Iriarte, what's wrong?" He looked like a truck had run over him more than once. "What happened?" Alma was already feeling sorry for him; his handkerchief looked limp with the tears he was wiping from his cheeks.

"Alma, you are Blanquita's friend. Please, by God, tell me where she is going."

"Ay, Señor, what happened?" Alma grimaced thinking how much her friend hated that name.

"She left, gone. I don't know where." He was wringing his hands now. Lala stroked his forearm as he began to sob. "My daughter, my daughter."

"Oh, this is terrible, Señor," Alma was determined to mislead them both in advance of her own escape.

Loly's father's chest caved in as Lala asked him to please come in and sit inside where the heat was not so bad. "Please, niña, tell this poor father anything you know."

He wearily repeated the message from his daughter's farewell letter, shaking in his hands; great heaves interrupted his telling. "She says she was too young to marry." He reached his outstretched hand to Lala. "That we don't understand her. My own flesh and blood!" He wiped his face with a different handkerchief. "I wouldn't have made her do it, Señora, I swear. I was only looking for her well-being but may God strike me down now, I wouldn't have made her if I knew she would run away."

"Señor, I can't believe Loly would do such a thing." Alma pushed out little indignant tears while turning from one elder to the other. "She is my best friend." She brought her hands to cover a pretend-quivering mouth. "It is only now from you that I learn of this disaster." Alma willed her face to redden. "I thought we were friends!"

"Niña, do you know anything that can help them find her?" Lala grabbed her hand and squeezed. Alma turned away, looking instead into the man's watery eyes.

"I'm so very sorry, Señor," she sniffled before exhaling deeply. "It pains very much to say that I don't know anything."

And they believed her.

WHO KNOWS BEST

His niece's boyfriend, being thirty and never married, with no children, a good dresser and well groomed, had to be gay; he was sure of it. Just listening to Becky go on and on about him, he thought, la pobre, she's such a good girl but absolutely and utterly innocent. Vicente took it upon himself to set his family straight, sort of speak. He sat the twenty-two year-old down one afternoon when the rest of the clan were looking at the photos from the twenty-five year-old's recent wedding, a wedding he refused to attend because he wasn't permitted his plus one. They had all long ago "accepted" him but not his partner; he still wasn't sure if it was more racial than sexual but Jimmy's dreds and six-foot-three frame were what drew him in the first place.

"Mamita, do you really know much about this guy?" A Colombian or Chilean who worked on cruise ship and was conveniently gone six days out of seven.

"Tío, we talk for hours; he's very serious and formal." She bit her trembling lip, a little teary-eyed now. "He respects me, tío . . . I love him." Now her makeup was smeared and she was weeping. Vicente hugged her and decided to take it up with his sister, the mother of this naive little creature. He thought she'd listen if he called her at work where there were no distractions from her crazy household. She had to listen; she was, after all interested in grandchildren.

"Hermana, I need to warn you about Becky's boyfriend," he spoke with confidence.

"No, what? Qué pasa?" She sounded engaged.

"Have you spent time with him? I think . . ." He let it hang there a moment. "I wonder if you know anything about him."

"What, Vicente? Have out with it, already." Her big sister-bossy attitude struck a nerve. First born, light of their parents' lives, perfect daughter who produced perfect children—the only grandchildren they'd get; Vicente could never measure up.

"Well, I hate to say it, Tati, but I am pretty sure this guy is gay."

"What the hell are you talking about? Are you stupid? Why would you say that?"

It was almost as if she forgot for a moment. Just one moment.

BIG DIFFERENCE

The boy I wanted, wanted someone else. That's not even the messed up part. See, he fell for me, or I thought he did, when he was broken up with her. Again, this isn't the crazy thing. Turns out I look like her. Yea, that's the crazy part. He had been away from her for like a year and then meets me and we clicked. I mean like, connected like those nuisance love bugs swarming around here—stuck together, floating all over the place in the throes of mating, you can't open your mouth for fear of swallowing a bunch. Mami says they're indecent, but I'm getting ahead of myself. And it doesn't help that I fell for him even before I met him. Not your run-of-the-mill broken hearts romance. That's why I have to tell it. Sort of like a warning story.

It started in high school. I had a friend who was the envy of all the girls—best hair, cutest clothes, frigging amazing makeup. Everyone wanted to be like her; she had curves angled just the right way and a charming little ass she swayed just so in the latest jeans. She was a friend of convenience—at least I was to her because I had a car but I didn't care because to me she was a lifesaver. I hadn't fit in with the in-crowd but when Marcela, even her name was cool, when Marcela's family moved from up north into the house next door, it was like fate. It's not like my car was anything special either; it was what it was supposed to be—a big hunk of metal with wheels that got me places and sometimes the air conditioner worked fine but most of the time I had to roll down the windows to let the blasting wetness that is a South Florida breeze move around and frizz my hair to no end. Marcela didn't like it when the air wasn't working either because she went through a whole lotta trouble to get her hair straightened flat like a China. She even dyed it jet black; I think she liked it when I called her Chinita. Big joke because her eyes're way round and mines're almond-shaped. Papi used to call me his chinita but now he just calls me mamita, if he talks to me at all.

Marcela talks really fast. Sometimes I can't keep up. She says girls in Florida talk like hicks and I know she means to include me but doesn't want to hurt my feelings so when she criticates—our Spanglish for criticar and criticize—she'll add, "but you're different." Nice of her but I don't believe much that comes outta her mouth. Even though I was born in New Jersey and that's one of the things she considers superior to being born anywhere else, including Cuba. I don't remember nothing because I was three when we moved to Florida. But it doesn't matter anyway because I am happy to be in her company and chauffeuring her wherever she wants to go so that some of her coolness will rub off on me.

We cruise the parking lots of high schools that have cuter guys than ours, Hicksville-freaking-high. I wish I had gone to the catholic school my cousins go to in South Broward but my parents can't afford all three of us there—"We can't just send one," mami said but in my heart I wish they had made the exception for me, the oldest and only girl. What the hell did my brothers care anyway? They were jocks—basketball freaking day-and-night since papi put that hoop on the front of the house; the pounding, hitting and bouncing made me want to tear that shit down. But Fredi and Nick usually treated me ok; they weren't in my business and to tell the truth, they are really good players— eleven months apart—a lot of people thought they were twins. Might as well've a been, they looked so alike. They wouldn't have gone to the catholic school anyway because they were hot shot superstars at the middle school. And they didn't need anyone because they had each other. But mami said no, public school for all three of us though I bet I coulda made papi let me.

I was about to start junior year, depressed at facing the same stupid faces in all my classes, hating my hair, my clothes and wishing I could just quit when papi bought me an old school tank of a car—a baby blue Lincoln. He was grinning, saying it was a classic.

"Mija, what do you think? It's beautiful, verdad?" He was petting it like a racehorse or something.

"Wow," was all I could offer. He went nuts showing me all the buttons and things he fixed.

"Mira, mi china, this is for cassettes and I put a lock on the gas tank." Papi liked cars and was always buying junkers, fixing them up and then selling them. I had no idea he had gotten this for me; until then, he let me drive his pickup on the way to school when he was going to his job at the garage and mami would get me afterwards though she didn't like for me to drive her car. I had already stopped buying cassettes and was collecting CDs but I didn't mention it.

"Papi," I spoke slowly, careful not to hurt his feelings, "it's so big."

"Exactly. I want a big car to protect you; anybody crashes into this is gonna feel it. You'll be safe." He offered the keys;

the keychain had a fluffy pair of dice with the Cuban flag on all sides.

"Wow. Ok."

"Vamos. Let me see how you handle this."

We drove to the beach and back and to be honest it really did feel solid, the gas pedal smoothly accelerating and the brake was even softer; little taps slowed that big motherfucker down on a dime. Looking at Papi, I had to smile too because he was so happy and I thought I can handle high school another year with this ride.

Then Marcela and her family moved into the house next door that was trashed by the stoners mami called the cops on. Me and my brothers could get high just standing in the side yard. The bank sent a crew to clean it up and within a month, just days before school started, the moving van parked out front. The first sign of my salvation was a canopy bed.

A girl, finally! Turns out it wasn't Marcela's bed but her parents'—her mother was some kind of decorator. The inside of their house changed every few months; her mom would get to moving furniture, painting, sewing curtains or draping material, all sorts of tricks I admired. I even encouraged mami to consider asking for help.

"For what? I like my things the way they are." She was not sure she liked my hanging out there so much but Marcela didn't have any brothers and her dad worked nights.

"I don't want you there if he's home; let the man have peace and quiet in his own house without you girls making noise."

But I knew it had more to do with the fact that he was a man. Mami didn't trust men.

Marcela told me stories about all the people she used to

hang with back in West New York, New Jersey, which everyday sounded more and more like where I should have grown up instead of bumfuck North Dade, Florida.

"The record stores back home have all the albums they play in the clubs, not the radio shit," Marcela claimed. The only record store near us just had rock, metal, punk, country and a little R & B—not much variety. Their CD selection was pitiful.

"And where the hell are the boutiques here?" Marcela spoke with an authority that was impressive even though I knew she hadn't been all over town yet. "Boutiques aren't cloned, ok? Nothing like the 5-6-7 stores. . ."

Laughing, I interrupted with a correction, "you mean 5-7-9 . . ."

"Whatever. You know what I mean. Where are the designer clothes and shoes, really cutting edge stuff? Styles that haven't come out in the American magazines yet, you know?" She knew a lot about fashion, subscribed to *Vogue*—the American and French versions—which we'd pour over every month.

Marcela said the boys in her old high school were fine. She said, "fiiiinnnee," like the black girls said it. A lot of times, she sounded like a black girl; another reason I wanted to go to New Jersey.

So, back to the boy that got away, who was never mine to begin with; his full name was José Danilo Pérez but everybody called him Danny and he was one of those Marcela said was especially fiiiiinnee.

Her name, the girl he left me for who was the girl he left in the first place, was Elena Sánchez. Everyone called her Elly. The good girl that got him in the end.

Marcela told their story, how they were high school

sweethearts for freshman and sophomore years and, "they were so cute," because they had even been "going out" in grammar school (that's what she said they call every grade from kindergarten to eighth in Jersey). Elly and Danny, Danny and Elly became the melded Danielly and they were always together until they weren't when he broke it off. I never did learn why; maybe that's part of the lesson here.

The summer after they split, Danny came down to Florida with his boys to hang out on South Beach. This was before it was trendy, way before Versace got shot. Most of it was still more of a dive then, good and cheap for families from up north to spend the factory-laid-off-weeks at these old run down hotels right on the beach or across Collins. Now none of them go for less than a couple hundred a night. But back then a bunch of guys would rent a room, everybody pitching in and pack in ten or more, throwing mattresses on the floor raising all kinds of hell for weeks.

I met Danny by the pool of the Delano; he came over to say hello to Marcela who had already filled me in on his life story and how cute he was. Wavy brown hair and caramel-colored eyes, tanned, beautiful bright teeth and so fiiinnne I could hardly stand it. Sure was. And to my surprise, he was into me. So much that we were exclusive for the rest of the summer, getting hot and heavy up to a point. Marcela was a little surprised too but happy because she had a thing for Danny's best friend Tito and so we all got to spend a lot of time together. Every morning, she and I would speed down I-95, cross over the causeway without the tolls and lay out on the beach until the guys woke up and found us. Usually there'd be an outdoor tea dance at one of the hotels along South Collins in the late afternoon and then afterwards Marcela and I'd go home to change and come back at night to hit the little clubs hidden in the same hotels until curfew, the ones with no cover and lax on IDs. By late August I couldn't think of anything but Danny, morning, noon, night and in my dreams, when I could sleep. While Marcela and Tito were not thinking beyond summer, I was scheming how to get myself to Jersey when Danny was gently chewing on my bottom lip. It was like all of my senses were in hyper drive around him. Sometimes he'd breathe into my ear and I'd feel my whole body tremble, leaving me with an aching that required his soothing.

"You're amazing," he'd say, but I didn't need to hear it.

"I want to be with you all the time." I didn't have to say it back for him to see my complete devotion.

"You gonna come visit me in Jersey?" If he only knew that I was already calculating the cost of a Christmas getaway—my aunt, mami's sister Ana whose daughter was a year younger than me lived not far from Danny. Perfect excuse.

Summer vacation was almost over, senior year about to start and Danny, Tito and the guys piled into their busted up Oldsmobile and headed back north. There was a word in English, better than any word I could find in Spanish that described how I felt—bereft. Marcela was sad and all but she hadn't put so much of herself out there with Tito. But not me. I was bereft because I handed Danny the key, the lock and my whole self—everything but my cherry. And I'm not gonna lie to you, I did so willingly, and easily because his grip on me was that tight. But like I said right at the beginning, he chose her.

I started writing letters—this was before email and cell phones were easy. To call him, I had to gather up a bunch of change for a public phone, yea, they still had them back then. I couldn't call from home because my parents would freak if they knew I was pining for some dude in New Jersey who didn't have the decency to even come to the house to meet them. I had already planted a seed about Christmas break.

"I wanna go see my cousin Yesenia and tía Ana. It's been so long and I'm saving my money to pay my own ticket. I want to see snow!" I dropped that little nugget in late September after I started working at the fast food joint near school, taking on as many hours as I could without letting my grades slip.

"Snow? Estás loca?" Mami and papi laughed at that. "Mija, that's nice that you want to see la familia. They will be so happy to have you. Your papi and I can't afford such a vacations with all of us but I'm glad you will go and spend time with your primita."

Papi said ok as long as I was back for New Year's.

"I don't want to start a new year without all my children by my side," he grabbed my face in his hands. I think he was even a little emotional. He'd been that way since he saw me naked. By accident. I was checking myself out in a full length mirror; my bedroom door was closed but my parents don't believe in locks inside the house. Nobody was home and I was looking real hard, noting everything from the neck down to the unruly bush between my legs, trying to imagine Danny seeing me full on the first time. I had Madonna on loud so I didn't hear papi. And I didn't know how long he'd been standing there looking. When I finally noticed, my hands dashed to cover whatever they could but I couldn't move. He freaked worse than me, eyes wild and hands crazy while saying, "I'm sorry, mija, I'm sorry, I'm so sorry."

We never mentioned it and I think that's why he didn't protest my going to el norte. And Marcela was going with me;

that was another condition. I was beyond psyched. I had already been on a plane before when we went to Abuelo Felo's funeral in Newark but I was only nine. Marcela was going to stay at her aunt's house in Union City and I'd be a twenty minute bus ride away in Jersey City.

"What do you expect?" Marcela asked me after we had gotten our tickets. The question knocked me down.

"What do you mean?" I tried not to sound as shaken as I felt.

"What do you think is gonna happen when you see Danny?" Seemed like she wanted to prepare me, but for what I wasn't sure. She had seen his little letters (there were two and never more than a half page while mine were three pages front and back). He wrote about his crappy job, school, his little brother's breaking his leg, how he hadn't seen Tito in weeks and then, at the end, there'd be a line or two about putting his hands all over me and what he wanted to do to me. This always made me and Marcela laugh our asses off; it was like he was two different people. The first guy was a pen pal-stranger bullshitting and then this other guy, the player trying to get with me by any means possible. Marcela agreed we belonged together too and made a cuter couple than him and Elly, but she neglected to say, not once did it cross her mind to tell me how much I looked like her.

Never saw that coming. I wasn't even worried about long-distance love or my parents not knowing anything about him or even Danny's plans on going to dental school in the DR. I would wait because I had made him my man. Then I learned that no matter how long I waited, he'd never be mine because I was a stand-in for her. I was in a competition with her and never knew it.

After all the shit went down, Marcela decided to show me a picture she had all along in her last yearbook. Like it just fucking occurred to her. I seriously studied that black and white portrait of Elena "Elly" Sánchez. Her glossy black hair looked thick even though it was cut short like a boy's but she could pull it off because her face was nice, cute little nose and eyes even more chinita than mine. Her cheekbones seemed to shine without blusher and lips to die for, damn it. The blurb underneath read "Elena Sanchez, Sophomore Year Sweetheart! Better half of Daniely." How the hell could I compete with that? I was utterly invisible in my high school before Marcela arrived—even though I was actually glad about that because it was populated with geeks, stoners and jocks. But what would I have given to have been in a school like Marcela's packed with fiiiineeeeness?

When I met Danny, my black hair was super short, within an inch of my scalp and I'm not conceited or nothing but papi always, always said I was a pretty child and mami said I was lucky enough to stay that way after the pimples and baby fat melted off. Maybe the reason papi didn't look at me anymore was because the pretty little child was gone. If you looked at that photo of Elena and looked at me, anyone'd think we were sisters or at least cousins. That Marcela didn't see it is another story.

"You're way smarter and have a nicer body than her," Marcela tried to comfort me.

"But he picked her."

Looking at that photo after it was all over made everything clear. I saw the little differences between us but by that time I knew what the biggest difference was and it wasn't something you could see.

to tell him.

By the time Marcela and I were flying back to Florida we had both given it up. She didn't have to tell me because I could see it in her face even before she started boo-hooing as the plane pulled away from the gate. I had never seen her cry.

"Oye 'Cela, what's the matter?" I leaned over to get close to her. We had three seats to ourselves and it was my turn to be next to the window.

She sniffled and rubbed her face into her sleeve, smearing her mascara and eyeliner. After a minute, she spoke but it was too soft to hear above the airplane noise. My ears were already popping. I shook my head and mouthed "I can't hear nothing."

She tried louder but not loud enough for the people in front or behind us to hear.

"Tito." She gulped and sniffled some more. "Tito and me did it." Her hands shot up to cover her face.

"Pero why you crying?" I rubbed her forearm closest to me. I hadn't planned on telling my story; I wanted to keep it to myself like a delicious secret I could taste over and over until I saw him again.

"But I shouldn't of." She looked around to make sure no one was looking. No one was. "He said he loved me but I know he doesn't. He has a girl."

"What?" We both knew Tito wasn't the boy scout-type but that's kinda why she liked him. "Are you fucking kidding me?"

"No, my friend Lety told me." Marcela sniffled some more, cleared her throat then looked me dead in the eye. "And Danny's slick with Elena."

A big pocket of air blew up in my throat and I started shaking,

The December Marcela and I went north, it was fifteen degrees when her uncle Eddie picked us up at the airport. I had never been so cold in my entire life and didn't have the right clothes for such a shock. Tía took me to Secaucus for a wool coat, "My Christmas gift to you, niña, so you don't get pneumonia. Your mother'd kill me if something happens to you."

The dry air flattened out my hair but it still stood on end. My chapped lips split and my knuckles were raw. I had to take my cousin everywhere; she was the excuse to visit but she got in my way. Yesenia wanted to go to the movies in Journal Square and I wanted to stay on the bus to Union City so I gave her ten bucks to spend on candy and told her to watch the movie through twice. I wanted to surprise Danny the first time I saw him. Marcela found out he was working in the bodega on North Bergenline. She met me at the corner and we walked in together. He was stacking cans when he looked up at me after a few seconds.

"What the . . ." Danny was blinking and stammering. He finally stood up, almost knocking his stack down, and hugged me. No kiss, just a little half-assed hug. I sure wasn't expecting that. He moved us away from the aisle towards the back, away from the manager's view.

"Oh my God, you're here. I can't believe it. You said so but . . ."

"Yep, I keep my promises," I said and I thought I saw his mouth twitch.

"Danny, you and Tito should take us out this Saturday. We'll be here until the thirtieth," Marcela stuck her spoon in it.

I couldn't keep my eyes off of him, searching for any little change (he'd lost his bronze tan and his hair was gelled and crunchy-looking). He kept catching my eye and then looking around and away. It was fishy.

"For sure, for sure. He's working at a catering hall. I'ma see if he can get the day off."

Marcela narrowed her big eyes a bit.

"Yea, I'm sure he can switch with someone. I gotta work til 6:00 on Saturday." Danny touched my arm and leaned in close to me so she wouldn't hear. "Baby, you look sooo good."

An electric shock shot from his lips to my ear, down my neck straight to my nipples. We had gone as far as him feeling me up under my bikini top in the ocean, his thing bumping and rubbing up against me freaked me out at first but I couldn't resist his arms tight around me. He was a fantastic kisser but that's only comparing him to the three boys I had kissed before with the standard being set by what I saw on TV (mostly closed mouthed) and the porn movie Marcela's father hid under his mattress (super sloppy and lots of tongue). I knew what steps there were and wasn't quite ready for it in the summer but now I felt primed and determined.

Marcela punched Danny in the arm stealing his attention from me.

"You better tell your friend to call me back. I left him like three messages," she somehow made it sound like it'd be his loss if he didn't.

"No doubt, I'll be sure to let him know," he said as he touched my upper arm but I had so many clothes on, the electricity couldn't flow. I couldn't help myself so I leaned over and kissed him on the lips, soft and fast. He grinned and nodded toward the front, indicating that his boss was watching.

"Here's my phone at my aunt's house," I pulled out the paper I had carefully prepared with a number and names of my NJ

relatives. Marcela grabbed it and wrote her number on the back for Tito.

"No excuse now. He's got the digits and so do you," she winked at him. I was still biting my bottom lip aching to kiss him again and I did; I didn't give a shit who saw.

We did go out that weekend—to the movies with Tito Saturday and then Sunday just him and me and my co to a dance at the Cuban club; tía Anita thought it was a good idea" to take Yesenia to hear real old school m cubana. She was actually dressed kinda cute and I wouldn' minded sticking with her but as soon as Danny met us t abandoned my cousin just as someone asked her to dar slipped into the freezing night just through the metal do headed to his car where we made out slow and steady fo hour. Even though it was frigid outside, we got so hot car windows were steamed up with little ribbons of wa sliding down. He put his hand inside my panties and wetness he found there surprised me but not him.

"We gotta get outta here," he said afterwards group of kids coming toward us. Even with my ey could tell they were going to the dance by the sor shoes. I was in some kind of dreamy, swoony state. I forehead, nose and chin while he carefully pushed from my face. It wasn't really a word I answered w a cross between a moan and an affirmative.

"Fix your dress, babe." He was buttoning and if you killed me right now I couldn't tell you anyt car except that hanging from the mirror he had dice like the keychain papi gave me but I neve trying to breathe. Somehow I stood, climbed over Marcela and rushed up the aisle only to be blocked by the stewardesses and their humongous drink cart. By the time I made my way to the back of the plane, I was gasping for air and the people waiting in line for the toilet were so freaked they let me through. As soon as I locked that door, I felt crushed, as if the tiny walls were what was squashing my chest. The air was sickly sweet and thin—as much as I wanted to take in a deep breath so I could scream, I couldn't. I splashed and splashed onto my burning face as much of the trickle of water released by my furious pounding on the knob but it didn't matter because when I finally saw myself in the mirror I was even redder than papi when he saw me.

OTHER PEOPLE'S HOMES

M y mother didn't like for me to go into other people's homes. I never understood it until she broke her own rule. It all started with my father. He used to work in a bus depot. I'm not sure what his job was but I remember he used to bring home all sorts of things that people had left on buses— umbrellas (we had tons of them), magazines, books, sometimes jackets or sweaters. To this day I guess what he did involved cleaning the buses.

Where my father worked was in the Jersey City terminal; he had the night shift. My mother worked days sewing. They traded off taking care of me and my brother, Carlos, who is younger than me. Sometimes my mother would drop my brother off at my father's job so that he could hang out with him and "see where papi worked." It was a greasy, dark place. Diesel stink everywhere. Buses parked close together all around. My father and brother would eat takeout food together—usually Chinese pepper steak. Mami and me would go do errands and end up eating at a counter somewhere in McKinley Square. These were the times when we ate something American. Stuff my mother would never cook like fried chicken, meatloaf, Salisbury steak or something weird like that. When we were done going to the bank or the bodega, mami and me would pick Carlos up. He was always sheepish after his dinners with papi (I didn't know what sheepish was then but when I looked it up, I knew that it was exactly how my brother looked those times). I didn't feel cheated though. I didn't like being around all that grease and oil, that cavernous building. Though I liked going into the empty buses and running up and down the aisles or sitting up front behind the invisible driver. I got to do these things anyway when we'd drop Carlos off so I didn't mind going off with mami while he and papi ate with the "guys."

One of the guys my father worked with was named Al. I think he was a mechanic and he worked the same shift as papi. Apparently they became friends—as much as this was possible because my father's English was very broken and Al couldn't even try talking with him in Italian like some of the other guys because he was Polish (I remember this because his last name ended in ski). Al lived down the shore and commuted into the city every day. Al was always telling my father about his house and boat and how we should all go down there one weekend and stay over and go swimming. He invited us so many times that my father finally got around to telling mami. One night while we were eating dinner papi said, "Vamos, Julia, what harm could be done?" My eyes stuck low to the kitchen table. I saw my brother sticking green beans under his plate. Mami sighed as she lifted Carlos' plate and said, "Está bien, Mario; if you have your heart set on it, we'll go."

We left our small third floor apartment on a summer Saturday morning. The drive in our un-air-conditioned station wagon from the city to the shore was long and hot as we left the smokestacks, oil refineries and pumping stations behind us along the turnpike. Heat trapped pollution over the sky obscuring the tall buildings of downtowns along the way. Approaching the shore there was more and more land around. Where we lived there weren't too many empty lots; down there, wide open spaces with grasses, trees, swamps and rivers spread out on each side of the car.

We arrived at Al's house before noon. The first thing I noticed was that they had a mailbox. I knew what it was, of course, but I was surprised anyway. Our mail was deposited in a little metal door with a slit next to seven other metal doors in the front hall. As soon as we went inside, Al's wife had us sit down in the dining area and eat the tuna fish sandwiches she had prepared for us. My brother made a face but mami lifted her eyebrows and he bit into the sandwich with his eyes closed. While we ate, they told us how they had planned the day—a ride out on the boat, maybe some fishing or swimming and a barbecue later. I stared up at the high ceiling. Wood beams met in an upside down V. The walls were covered with wood paneling and there was a soft cushiony rug beneath us. They had two sofas, one facing the other, and a large strange driftwood lamp in a corner. On the wall directly opposite me there was a large map of the United States. I looked and looked for Jersey City but New Jersey was so small compared to the other states that I satisfied myself in finding New York City. There was only one other picture on the remaining walls; this one small but in a fancy gold frame, a seaside scene. I glanced toward the kitchen and saw a long counter with four swirling barstools pulled up to it. Their refrigerator even had a water and ice dispenser in the door. My mother noticed me looking around and told me, quietly, to finish my lunch.

They had two boys around my brother's and my age. They were pretty typical, I think, of North American boys—dirty blonde hair, light eyes and assertive. Before the introductions were all done the younger one asked Carlos if he wanted to play with his Hot Wheels track set. They were off before my mother could tell him in Spanish not to touch anything. The older boy, about ten, told me he had just gotten a chemistry set. My mother quickly shot me a threatening look lest I go with him but after she caught sight of papi nodding she changed her face to mean, "watch yourself."

Each boy had his own room. The one I went with, I think his name was Ethan or Josh, a name my parents could not pronounce, his room had bunk beds. At first I was confused because I hadn't seen any other children around. When I asked, Ethan or Josh said that he had friends sleep over all the time. None of my friends ever slept over nor was I ever allowed to sleep over anywhere.

Ethan or Josh was eager to show me the vials and powders and liquids. I was more interested in the model airplanes hanging from the ceiling and the human anatomical doll. The body had exposed muscles and you could pull pieces off to see bones and organs and veins. Ethan or Josh got bored with me pretty soon and grabbed a football and asked if I knew how to play. I lied and said no because I wanted to stay and look at all the books lined up above his desk; he even had his own lamp. He left and I ventured up into the top bunk. My mother came in to check on me and made me get down and go outside to see the canal behind the house.

Carlos and Scott (the younger one's name was easier to remember because one of the black kids in my class was named Scott Williams) were vrooming and crashing cars in the next room. They were pretty angry at being told to put the toys up and come outside.

Al had a boat tied to a post out back. Their yard had no grass but white gravel instead; placed all around were anchors, nets and buoys. Carlos and me almost immediately began throwing rocks in the water and Al's sons laughed at us. My dad and Al went into the boat and there was still room for all of us. Besides the Staten Island Ferry, this was the biggest boat we had been in. It had a canvas top and my mother and Al's wife sat underneath it to avoid the sun. Mami and Mary, that's Al's wife, had kerchiefs tied under their chins so their hairdos wouldn't get messed up. We children were told to sit down and stay down as the men untied the boat and revved the engine. We took a leisurely ride, looking at all the houses lining the wide canal. We entered a small bay where we got gas, bait and sodas. My father was the only one who caught a fish and Al patted him hard on the back and said that he brought him bad luck and wouldn't invite him fishing anymore. They all laughed and my father had a wide grin for the rest of the night.

I got to sleep on the top bunk and my brother slept on the bottom bunk in Ethan/Josh's room. Ethan/Josh slept in a sleeping bag in Scott's room. I had never seen one before. One of the sofas opened up into a bed and my parents slept there though Al and Mary offered them their bed but my mother wouldn't have it.

The next day we drove to a beach nearby and stayed there long enough for our noses and cheeks to get red. My mother wanted to go home before lunch but Al talked my parents into staying for a barbecue. They made hot dogs, hamburgers and corn on the cob. We were in the yard, sitting on benches around a wooden table when my brother asked for rice. Scott passed him a bowl full of coleslaw and said, "Nobody eats rice at barbecues, you dummy." I thought my mother would slap somebody because her face got all red. The brothers laughed and then their parents and finally my parents joined in but I could tell they didn't think it was too funny. Later Mary gave us all Good Humor ice cream bars. We didn't leave until dark so on the way back I didn't get to see the big open spaces, just little lights in the river as the boats steered along. Darkness hid the grass.

When we got home, the apartment felt all wrong. The picture of Santa Barbara with her shelf of candles and apples seemed to take up the whole wall. The plastic-covered lampshade looked tacky (another word I learned later). The refrigerator's single door seemed ancient. That night I fell asleep preoccupied with thoughts of rearranging the furniture in the living room. Maybe putting the sofa in the middle of the room and the TV against a different wall would make everything right.

I woke up the next day and stared out the window over my bed which faced the next apartment building's brick side wall only a few feet away. I realized then that the screen was thick with grime because it hadn't been cleaned since all the windows were painted shut. I leaned over to one side, cocking my head to see our backyard. It seemed too closed to share with seven other families. My eyes fixed on an overgrown thorn bush, its flowers long gone, the only adornment in that narrow rectangle of dirt. I had not noticed before.

DR. CUBANITA

"It takes so damn long to get anywhere in Florida," Lidia said, then bit her lip. Her boyfriend, mouth hung open, was sleeping in the passenger's seat. She stepped on the gas, revving the RPM gauge on the Swedish sedan to six thousand revolutions. Even before the halfway point on Alligator Alley, all the decent stations started scratching static, so she shut the radio off. In the quiet and desolation, she could appreciate the engine's steady hum. Manolo had fallen asleep as soon as they left Dade County and it was getting dark. She still had to finish her talk for the conference in the morning, but there were three hours driving at 85 mph left to get to Tampa, and she could feel the cramps twist in her abdomen. Just bleed, Lidia, what else could you possibly expect? She had had an abortion recently, at the ridiculous age of twenty-nine for God's sake, because the absurd diaphragm was too big or too small or out of place. That was in the spring, when she started seeing Manolo and she didn't even know if it was his or her ex-husband Sergio's. Pissed and pregnant, she never told either one and went by herself, just like she did when she was seventeen. That time she had lied to the nurse, saying her ride was waiting, not even telling her best friend Gladys because, well, Gladys was frigid. This time no one asked.

Lidia was now speeding past slower cars, returning to the

right hand lane once it was clear because the redneck troopers always nabbed the stupid ones in the left lane. Her eyes shifted from the shoulders of the road to the rearview mirror. Manolo's speed radar—it was Manolo's car—flashed a steady green, clear. Long, monstrous trucks thundered past in groups of twos or threes. Lidia drove, one slender manicured hand on the stick shift, the other fingering the leather-wrapped steering wheel.

The day projected itself onto the road, another crazy day with the crazies at the hospital. She had told Manolo she would drive, feeling sorry for his being "dead-tired," but so was she. Even though her supervisor, Stan, let her leave early, she still had to rush to the manicurist's then home to the house where she lived with her mother since the divorce, shower, change and pick up her bags. She had even packed a bathing suit, wishfully thinking there'd be time for St. Petersburg's lovely beach, but the damn paper, the shitty conference (she had yet to break into the national conference scene), the burning and twisting cramps and the radar—now beeping red—conspired to keep her from the calm, salty waters of the Gulf.

She took her foot off the accelerator, causing the too-close car behind to screech. Manolo shot up in his seat.

"Qué pasa?" he asked, his mouth still open.

"Nothing." She nodded toward two highway patrol cars in the low-lying grassy median.

"Mmm, good girl." He checked to see if her foot was on the brake. "Got an asshole behind you, eh?"

"Yea. Go back to sleep." She looked at his wide set, half-opened eyes.

"Have I been sleeping long?" He put his rough hand over hers atop the gearshift.

"I guess a coupla hours. Do you want to stop soon?"

"Do we need gas?" He yawned widely, switching the radio on at the same time then turning the knob left then right trying to find a station that wasn't country.

"No, we've got three quarters of a tank."

"I gotta pee, babe," he said grabbing his crotch.

She looked at him again, not half as handsome as her ex but not such a jerk either.

"I'll stop at the next rest area." They leaned together to kiss. He adjusted himself back in the seat. His heavy lids closed over the bright whites of his eyes and he was asleep within a minute.

Her mother hated Manolo—a lowly sub-contractor who laid tiles for Christ's sake—dating her daughter, the big shit psychologist, the doctor. But Manolo made thirty bucks an hour, was his own boss, hardly paid any taxes, and let her drive his nicest car, the "spare" that had once been his ex's. Lidia's cute little red Italian sports car, her father's last gift to her, was perpetually breaking down; she had parked it, indefinitely, out in the driveway since there was no room in the packed garage (her brother's motorcycle, sports equipment and trophies took up one side while the other was cluttered with the clothes and shoes her father had left behind—things her mother couldn't bear to part with).

Once the house had been a hub of excitement, representing her family's happy climb into the middle class. Now it felt sterile to Lidia. She passed quite a few nights alone, lying in bed, staring at the hems of the cream lace curtains swaying across the French doors in her room, thinking about her old life. It was not the room she had grown up in because, as a family, when they were still a normal family with a mother, father, brother and sister and a dog and a cat and four nice cars, before her father left them, even before he died, before her mother started getting depressed, before her brother moved in with an older woman, and before the dog died and the cat went blind, when her father's business made a ton of money in a couple of years, they had moved into a big custom built house in a trendy subdivision in South Dade.

Lidia and her mother had had a blast shopping for the new house. They combed through the pages of *Architectural Digest* and *Beautiful Homes* looking for ideas. Special attention was paid to every detail—more sophisticated lighting fixtures, better cabinets, marble counters, Italian ceramic tile throughout, shiny tables and carved chairs inlaid with ivory, an English crystal chandelier for the foyer, a deep Indian rug that made you want to get down on your hands and knees to feel it, a spa for six built into the patio, a fountain in the courtyard, skylights in the upstairs bathrooms, plus a Jacuzzi in her parents' bathroom. It was a beautiful house, the envy of all her friends from the private girls' high school because they lived in old houses in the Gables, houses with weathered red barrel tile roofs, wide arched doorways and old Cuban tiles in vaulted ceilinged rooms. Lidia's house had a sound system built into the walls, was zone- and climate controlled and had windows with discreet reflective glass. Though most houses in her cul-de-sac looked exactly alike from the outside, down to the impeccably landscaped plots in front, their house, the Duval home, her father's family had French ancestry, was different inside, different to the tune of an additional hundred thousand in decorating and furnishings.

She wondered how was it that she had so much to look back upon at so young an age. Her doomed marriage—short and long at the same time because they were engaged for so many years but wedded for only two—still perplexed her. She and Sergio had met at one of the small Catholic colleges in Miami, in a humanities class; their immediate and mutual attraction led to what she naively believed to be exclusive dating followed by a lengthy engagement lasting the duration of her grad school up north and culminating in a no-holds-barred wedding at the Biltmore that her semi-estranged father refused to pay for because her mother had raised all kinds of hell about his desire to bring his new love to the wedding. For her part, Lidia would have relished the opportunity to confront the gold-digger Colombian hussy, but as it turned out, the boon money dried up and her father had a massive heart attack two months before the wedding. At the eleventh hour, when the bridal shop would not release her designer gown and trousseau until the last installment was turned in and the hotel demanded to be paid in full, Sergio's parents gave them a check for $45,000 that, with Sergio's blessing, she promptly deposited in her super negative-balance bank account. Lidia immediately cut checks to cover all the bills standing in the way of her dream wedding. Her mother and her brother Guillermo Jr. walked her down the aisle, all three them crying and causing much of the bride's side of the church to tear up or sniffle sympathetically as they passed by. Sensing rather than knowing that it would be last time she, her mother and brother would be together, Lidia sighed deeply at the altar in delicious anticipation of her shiny new life with Sergio, oh-so-ready to begin once and for all.

She took her foot off the accelerator again, flipped the right indicator on and veered the car to the exit lane and towards the service plaza.

"You want me to drive now?" Manolo flipped the button on

the side of the seat to sit upright again.

"Didn't you want to pee?" She pulled into an empty spot close to the entrance and jerked the emergency brake up. "Think I'm getting my period."

"Oh, baby, hurry; go, go to the bathroom." He opened his door and then rushed over to get hers too.

"I need some change." She took the single and quarters he offered her and headed for the women's toilets where she did get her period, bright red blood flowing from an aching, bloated abdomen and belly she was determined to keep childless for the foreseeable future.

Lidia drove the rest of the way because, she told Manolo, it calmed her, let her think.

"Why do you need a freaking cappuccino machine when we get coffee every morning, Lidia?" Sergio grabbed the unopened box and slid it across the polished Italian granite counter in their neatly appointed, up-to-the-minute-outfitted kitchen in the newest gated community stretching ever more southwest of Miami. Sergio's lawyer father was in real estate and had gotten them their upgraded modern house. Lidia had enjoyed his family's favor for years while she dated then married their smart, but somewhat lazy son. A corner of her mouth turned up in a smile remembering how they thought she would be able to turn him around. But she couldn't change him, couldn't even see that he was sliding lower and lower while the blow kept him as witty and upbeat as usual. About a year into their marriage they stopped going to his parents' Spanish-style mansion in the Gables for Sunday brunch when Sergio's seven-years younger sister had identical twin boys—the first grandchildren. Sergio had wanted kids right away but Lidia, only two years out of grad school and fresh from an internship in a Pompano rehab for addicted teens, had just started working full-time.

On one of those Sundays, Lidia had been invited to help feed one of the twins, but no matter how much she politely refused, she was handed Julian, a burp rag and a plastic bottle holding a sleeve of formula, the nipple a dark, flat rubber circle topping a squat punctured cylinder.

"It's not so hard," Chela coaxed while Lidia nervously held the squirming child. "Just hold his head like this." She showed her with Joaquin, who greedily sucked away.

Lidia knew she was being carefully observed, making her and the baby even more agitated; she couldn't get Julian's head held correctly so he gurgled, spit up and required frequent burping, a process that freaked the hell out of her because she wasn't sure how hard to pat the baby's back, so he never completely expelled the offending air. Julian whimpered miserably then let out a wail that caused her mother-in-law to snatch him away and Sergio to shake his head. After that Lidia begged off the family Sunday brunches because of "required extra time at work" and Sergio bitterly agreed it was the best thing. Her once attentive mother-in-law stopped calling. By then Sergio's business was failing. He was getting home late and leaving early in the morning, such as the day he remarked upon the new coffee machine.

"We can use it on the weekends," she pointed out, but he was already waving his hand as he turned away. "Don't be a dick, Sergio. You like cappuccino."

Lidia had bought one of the first machines at Burdines, fascinated by the levers and steaming apparatus as the product demonstrator worked his seduction. Soon after their wedding, she used all the cash gifts and checks to buy the twelve setting Limoges china she had coveted. Never used, it was now stored in cushioned, zippered vinyl cases, along with the remaining detritus of her marriage, in a storage unit she was two months' behind on. Lidia had brought over $200,000 worth of debt into the marriage, $115,000 of it from grad school loans; the rest built up in a frenzy of spending she justified because of her sacrifice of living away from Miami for three years. Sergio forgave her for the student loans, paying them off as his groom's gift, but the rest of her debt had doubled by their first anniversary—a whole new wardrobe of working-professional clothes, weekly mani-pedis, salon-colored and cut hair, waxing of brows, chin and bikini-line: "Beauty costs a lot," she often told him. He agreed. But she didn't know that Sergio had had his own mounting debt, to his dealer, an old high school druggie-friend who kept him well-stocked with packets of the finest powder.

They made it to Tampa at eleven in the evening. Manolo fell into bed in the too cold room and rolled to one side for her. She tossed and turned, missing the swaying, dancing Belgium lace curtains.

On recent sleepless nights, the unbearably wearisome nights when she'd open the sliding glass door and let the air conditioning breathe into the dark dampness, Lidia would try to discover the origin of her mother's hatred of Manolo. It couldn't just be class; after all her mother was herself of working class stock, her grandfather a dairy farmer. Was it that Manolo was ordinary—but wasn't her seamstress grandmother ordinary? Or was it his dark skin, which her mother disapproved of, though Lidia found Manolo's naturally trigueño looks sexy.

Of course, her mother had adored Sergio, a lawyer, a "good" son of a rich old Miami-Cuban family. She blamed Lidia for his getting into drugs, his practice being shot to hell, his falling out with his family—the Lópezes of Coral Gables.

"If you had been a better wife," her mother had said.

Lidia slid spit between her teeth before saying, "He's a grown man and did exactly what he wanted to do."

"But you should have known," her mother said, almost whining.

"You should have known about daddy," Lidia said, cocking her head. Talking of their spouses led only to spiteful, stinging words with no resolution. Now she avoided her mother as much as possible; one passing glance from her—what with her long jaw and sidelong looks—always put Lidia's nerves on edge. She reminded her of a kind of pathetic-looking dog, but she couldn't think of the breed's name. Sometimes, Lidia just wanted to kick her but, naturally, she couldn't because her mother was pushing sixty and a widow and starting to drink a lot in the evenings. They couldn't even have a cafecito together without bickering so Lidia skipped it all; on the rare occasion when they did anything together—shopping, their once favorite pastime for instance—it was marked by a stifling tension that caused the bleached blonde hairs on her arm to stand on end.

At one in the morning, unable to sleep, Lidia got up and re-worked her paper while silently watching *Snows of Kilimanjaro* with a handsome young Gregory Peck. She thought about how lovely it would be to be able to go on a photo-safari in Africa. Trouble would be the bad food, unhygienic facilities and no air conditioning or maybe not even screens, and the danger, of course but, on the other hand, it probably would be exciting, exotic, something so adventurous none of the Coral Gables crowd would ever venture to try it.

At three in the morning, she shuffled her paper together and returned to bed, where Manolo was alternately snoring and wheezing.

When the sun shone in the room, Manolo woke her gently, tracing a finger along her shoulder. His benevolent gaze broke a smile onto her lips and for a moment they were very still. Lidia's eyes were attracted to the blinking digital clock. 7:18. She jerked the covers away.

"Shit, I'm going to be late!"

Lidia was miserable for most of the day, cramps grinding in her bloated gut and interminable talks where no one looked up from the podium except briefly when they had finished going on and on. She had marked sessions of interest in every time-slot, hoping to gain some insight about effectively treating the criminally insane, but the presenters' droning voices lulled her to stupor. Five cups of watery complimentary coffee and two 500 milligram painkillers later, she needed to go outside and bum a cigarette to perk up. There was a cold chicken-cordon bleu with a side of mushy vegetables lunch—she had been seated at a table with a trio of grad school buddies (not hers) and two older men, one with a full head of white fluffy hair and the other a striking bald black man with round frameless glasses. They were polite but disinterested in chatting so she fixed her eyes on the cherry-topped cheesecake and reviewing the conference program for afternoon sessions she could ditch. She wanted to be collegial, to be taken seriously, but knew that by the time of her session on

Sunday morning, most people would be sleeping in or have left the conference altogether.

More weak coffee was making the rounds as the keynote speaker was being introduced. Lidia had come to the conference because of her, a distinguished professor who edited a journal she desperately wanted to be published in. Lidia had submitted three essays, each rejected after a six-month's wait. She took out a pen and opened to the blank pages at the back of the program, ready to copy any wisdom or guidance she could ascertain. This scrutiny might reveal the key to getting onto a national panel or even getting published. Lidia tried hard to understand what made this woman's new research, and her off the cuff remarks, so special. After fifteen painstaking minutes, Lidia was bored and began mentally tearing apart the cheap, ill-fitting suit and horrible low-heeled pumps the frumpy, famed scholar was wearing—her up-do had scraggly hairs coming out at weird angles and not a single drop of makeup, not even lip gloss.

The next morning, they got up and ate a big breakfast of eggs, ham, grits, and biscuits with gravy and drank large cups of decent coffee at a diner far from the conference center. Lidia had slept heavily and late thanks to half a bottle of merlot, not caring about what she'd missed. Manolo reminded her of the book exhibit she'd wanted to see, so she arrived in time for the already paid for insipid lunch then spent time browsing the books, reading introductions, tables of content and especially the biographies of contributors—noting where they'd gone to school or previous publications. She'd worked herself up into the bitchiest of states by 3:30 and called Manolo to rescue her in time for them to catch happy hour in a beach front bar in

Clearwater.

The afternoon heat had dissipated after a sudden, intense thunderstorm and the beach was mostly empty but for a few Latin American tourists.

"So, you're not too into the conference stuff, eh?" Manolo handed her a double margarita on the rocks with too much salt as he set his own beer down on the high round cocktail table.

"It's a big shit." She licked the glass rim and took a big gulp. "I don't know why I bother," she sighed then blew out raspberries.

"Aw, babe, don't say that. You were looking forward to this." Manolo stroked her forearm. Her French manicured nails gleamed in one of the bar's haphazardly arranged spotlights. She stretched out both hands to admire them. She remembered how happy she had been with the big rock Sergio had given her—three and a half carat pear-shaped diamond set in platinum designed by a Palm Beach jeweler. That's when Lidia had started getting acrylics to better show her prize. But she had had to sell the ring to bail Sergio out the first time he got arrested. There was so much promise radiant in that ring, their marriage, so much to look forward to. Right up until then.

WHAT REMAINS OF MAX

Ok, so Sheila and I used to share an apartment down in Soho before it got so expensive that only depressing art types lived there. Max lived with us. Sheila wasn't a terrible roommate but she wasn't a very good one either on account that she is flaky and a lot of time she wouldn't come home to do dishes or laundry when it was her turn and she definitely wasn't a very good cat-owner because she'd forget to clean out Max's cat box or change his water or pour more food in his bowl. Now me being her best friend, I forgave her lots of stuff like leaving the counter top full of coffee grounds when she left in the mornings and borrowing my favorite Irish fisherman's sweater that Nicki got me without her asking, but she's my best girlfriend and, hey, I'm not perfect either.

But what really got me going was that damn cat box. It pissed Max off too. You see, Max wasn't like any other cat I'd ever known and I know everyone always says that animals are so much like people but that's bullshit. This cat was evil. I mean, I really think he was possessed. Max stalked Sheila. If she didn't come home at night, he'd sleep in the hall by the door until her keys woke him up and then he'd jump from the top of the bookcase onto her neck when she'd walk through the door. Sheila's funny though; she thought he was glad to see her. Well, he was. You see, I don't think Sheila really noticed that he was glad she was back so he could punish her for being so flaky. He'd scratch at her ankles when she walked by and he'd whine and whine that way Oriental cats do but Max was no Siamese; he was a huge orange and white striped sucker. He could be dog for all he weighed. Ate like one too.

Anyway one day, Sheila met Mark and she said she fell in love (I say "said" because Sheila's always falling in love with people and things and she used to always tell Max she loved him too but I know Max didn't buy it). Of course Max hated anyone Sheila brought home, thought he was being usurped or something, but he really had it out for Mark. Mark had a loft in the East Village and, of course, Sheila up and left again but this time for good. She packed up all of her stuff one Saturday afternoon while I was in Jersey visiting my family and when I came back, sure enough she was gone and Max was there. Now Sheila and I had a good friendship. She stayed outta my shit and I stayed outta hers and though she didn't clean the cat box every other day like she should have and wasn't around much to hang with, I still thought she was alright and I was happy she had found her prince from the East Village. But this Max thing irritated me.

I called her. "Sheila, sweetie, what's with Max?" But I guess I already knew then that she wasn't gonna take him.

"Clara, Max hates Mark. I don't know what to do. Every time Mark sleeps over, Max sits on the nightstand and gives him the evil eye. He puked onto his cashmere coat the other day. Besides, Mark's allergic to cats."

Excuses, excuses, but that's Sheila. She didn't dog me for sleeping till noon, or talking long into the night or my skeleton collection (they're mostly skulls, but not human) or even my annoying little habit of bathing (not showering, I like bubbles) twice a day. Sheila was chill; the best roommate for me, really. But this Max thing, well, I was worried 'cause he definitely knew she had abandoned him. When I got back from Jersey he was pacing, barely looked up at me. I swear if he coulda lit a match he'd have torched the place.

"Ok, so, you want me to keep him?"

"Oh, Clara, love of my life, you would be a saint to keep him. I mean I had the most morbid thought to put him ... God, it was a horrible thought, I mean it's Max. Max, my great big sweet putty cat ... " About now she's boo-hooing her eyes out and Max is whining and I'm feeling sorry for both of them.

"Ok, honey, I'll keep him. I wouldn't, ah, I couldn't, don't you worry, I'll keep him. He pretty much takes care of himself, you know."

"Clara, Clara, you're a peach. I promise you I'll pay for his food and litter and shots. I mean, it's the least I can do. I'll come by and see him too so he won't get too depressed."

Depressed? I wouldn't have used that word. He was spiteful. He knocked the water all over the kitchen so the floor was slick and I fell on my ass at night when I got up to drink something. He'd stuff his face until he was ready to barf and then he'd propel his cud at a strategic site such as the futon sofa or the Mexican leather chair. He did some nasty stuff with his little cat turds that I don't even want to talk about; just take my word for it, it was nasty. Anyway, he was bent on revenge but trouble is his main target wasn't around. He worked himself into such a state of agitation that I had to warn Sheila not to come over because I was sure Max'd kill her.

She did come over one time though and Max heard her voice

in the hall and his hackles stood straight up. I managed to lock him into the bathroom but the whole time she and Mark were there, Max slammed his fat body against the door. Eventually he broke the hook and lounged toward Mark's leg. Tore his raw silk pants and made a gash in Mark's leg the size of a serrano chili. I tell you this cat was bad.

For the most part, Sheila and Mark were happy little love bugs in their lovely little loft and me and my lover Nicki had to deal with this deranged cat. I kept out of Max's way mostly 'cause my mother always told me to stay away from obviously crazy people and, Max, well, like I said before, he wasn't just any animal.

Maybe Max was an ex of Sheila's in a past life or something. You know, like maybe Max and Sheila had been this great couple in history like Anthony and Cleopatra or Samson and Delilah but probably Sheila had abandoned Max in this other life too and he killed her or maimed her. That's my theory anyway.

Well, after a not so long but very bitter winter Max died. He just croaked. But he did it with style. He managed to find the only damn thing Sheila had left in the apartment, a bath rug; actually it was the U-shaped rug that goes around the toilet. Well, he kinda curled up in it and when Nicki got up to pee in the morning Max was dead, like a cat tamale.

Freaked me out. I poured salt all around Max's cadaver to ward off any bad Karma but I shoulda known that wouldn't help. I called Sheila but, as usual, she wasn't home—Mark was getting to know just how flaky Sheila could be.

"Whoa, Max died?" His voice kinda cracked.

"Yea . . . Will you tell Sheila to call me the minute she comes in?"

"Ok, but what are you going to do?" Mark spoke really quietly.

"I don't know. That's why I need Sheila to call me. Will you please tell her it's an emergency? I mean, I don't want, God, I can't have Max dead here."

"Ok, Clara, I'll, ah, tell her as soon as she gets back but, ah, the last time she left she was gone for a couple of days."

I knew then she had spaced out on Mark and she probably wouldn't be going back anytime soon so I would have to deal with this huge dead cat wrapped in a toilet rug surrounded by salt in my bathroom.

I called my mother and she said I should bury him but where the hell do you bury a cat in Manhattan? Do you carry a cat cadaver on the A train up to Central Park? Can you get a bus transfer while you're holding a stiff Max? No way.

My friends at work said I should just put him in the dumpster. They thought I was crazy for not just throwing him away. But who could throw away a body, I mean, it's not just a body, it's Max and he wasn't just an animal. Jesus, he coulda been Mark Anthony. I couldn't just throw him away. Nicki said to call the Humane Society and I did and then it was settled. Max would be cremated. Now I was brought up Catholic during the time when Catholics didn't get cremated and though it's cool now, I still felt a little weird about it but Nicki assured me it was a sacred practice and all so I was convinced. I decided to walk and carry Max to the Humane Society because it wasn't too far and, well, it was more dignified than a wild ride in a cab driven by some maniac.

I got there expecting to go to a ceremony I guess 'cause when the receptionist said she'd call me when it was over I was let down. I mean, I thought there would be some Humane Society ritual or something but nothing. Just, we'll call you when it's over.

I walked to work. My friends at the store thought I was going off the deep end but, hell, they didn't know Max. He had died heartbroken. I wouldn't want to die with a broken heart but you don't get to choose that, do you?

Well, the next day just as I was leaving for work I get the call.

"This is the Humane Society. It's over ..."

Before she could finish I cut her off, "I'll be right over."

It was stupid but I just headed over there. I still hadn't heard from Sheila and now I was going over there and I didn't know why. Well, of course, when I got there the receptionist remembered me and said, "You're here to claim the ashes of your cat."

I kinda nodded but internally I thought no way, I'm not doing this, am I really?

She was back in less than a minute with a dark plastic bag. It was a big bag and it had a strip of masking tape on it where someone had written "Max ashes"—I swear I'm not making this up. I actually smiled, for a second.

She asked me to sign a form and handed the big dark bag to me. It weighed a freaking ton. I swear it was like, excuse me, are you sure someone's Saint Bernard isn't in here too? I mean, Max was fat but shouldn't he weigh less now that he's been burnt to a crisp?

I guess I must have had a really weird look on my face because the receptionist felt like she had to ask me if I was all right.

All I could say was, "You sure this is Max?"

She started babbling; I think, anyway, 'cause all I heard was that the animals were cremated together but not really together so they could separate them and know which one was which and, like I said, the rest I don't remember. All I do remember was walking to work, crossing Houston Street with a cold wind in my face and crying and struggling to carry this heavy bag and trying very hard not to drop Max ashes.

I guess I was talking to myself while I was walking back to work 'cause nobody bothered me and they even got out of my way. I musta looked pretty crazy 'cause my friends saw me through the store window and were cracking up by the time I walked through the door delirious.

Sheila got in touch with me about a week after and told me she was moving out to California with a cousin of hers. She said she'd send for Max's ashes so she could bury him out there in the land of sunshine and stars. "Sure thing," I said but I knew I'd have to keep Max with me like Pilate kept her daddy's bones in that book Nicki was always talking about Solomon something. I couldn't abandon him now, I mean I didn't throw him away before, I wasn't going to do it now.

Nicki said we'd take him to Jersey and bury him there but we never did. Nicki was the one with the car and now we don't see each other anymore. Max's ashes are somewhere deep in the hall closet behind some boots I never wear so as not to disturb him. The last thing I need is to be haunted by a deranged cat.

LIKE A DOG

My dog is dying; he's old—fifteen—and big—110 lbs., so nobody ever expected him to last this long. He's a good boy. Of course, a member of the family—we got him from a neighbor whose collie bitch got knocked up by a roaming rottie or dobie (Buddy has the red/tan colors but his mama's long snout and legs). I took Buddy with me when I left home—well, when I got kicked out. I was nineteen and mami thought I was freeloading because I wasn't helping her out with the house but mostly because we got into a big fight.

"My nerves are shot since your father abandoned me." Mami throws out that line with stunning regularity.

Well, technically he abandoned us. Furthermore, it was ten years ago but I don't bring it up, again.

"I can't go to work, take care of you three and the house and cook and everything. It's just too much for one human being."

This is when I started bowing the invisible violin. By then my sister, the oldest, a sous-chef, wasn't even eating at the house and my brother, the baby, was still in high school and got away with murder just because he's male. Me, I was in school, had a work study and part-time, paid my own car insurance, cleaned my room and did everybody's damn laundry. But when she said that I should clean Dariel's room, that was the straw that broke my back and went up my ass.

So I booked it and took Buddy, a sweet mutt everybody loved. She never forgave me for that. It's probably why she's giving me such a hard time now about his dying.

"Why don't you put that poor dog down? Don't you think he's suffering?"

Buddy never complains, ever. This spring he slowed down, so instead of jogging together, we walked. Then he stopped eating his usual dry food. So I bought him canned food—different types to see which he liked. After a month or so he couldn't swallow that, I lost it. I starting giving him soup with rice and malanga (the tuber that's mami's cure for everything). But this week Buddy isn't eating anything and I was stupid enough to tell her.

"How can you let him die like that?"

"It's nature. He's going on his own terms." I couldn't stop crying and even when I wasn't crying, big fat tears just fell out of my eyes. Plop, plop, plop.

"Are you going to do the same thing to me? What if I have a heart attack or something and get hooked up to a million tubes being kept alive? Are you going to let me suffer?"

"Don't worry, ma. I will make sure to pull the plug."

I lie down next to Buddy and wait.

BARBIE DOLL

Whenever I remember P.S. 7, I remember Vanesa Simon, but I don't think she was at my school since kindergarten, like the rest of us neighborhood kids. I sort of remember her intrusion, that's what I felt it was, in about the third grade. Our school was a big old one with an olive green basement where all the classes lined up for the first bell and raising of the flag when it was raining or too cold outside. The three-story building took up a quarter of the whole block. I went there from when I was five till I graduated from the eighth grade. I lived half a block away. Vanesa lived near the park, where the new houses were.

When we were little we were friends though very mismatched ones. I'm not sure how we became friends, but maybe it was because the teacher assigned her to the desk next to mine. She was everything I was not—pale with dirty blonde hair, blue eyes, long legged. And she was rich. I guess if her family had been religious they would have sent her to Catholic school. Her father was Greek and her mother used to be a model so they probably didn't think it was right to send their golden child to St. Mary's, where you had to wear those queer plaid uniforms. She wouldn't have been able to show off all her clothes. And she had a lot of clothes.

Vanesa had a little sister and I a little brother. I think our kid sister and brother were in the same grade, just as Vanesa and I were. But her little sister, I can't remember her name now, never caused such a fuss as Vanesa did. Vanesa was different. Maybe it goes back to her being blonder than her sister or something, although they were both taking modeling classes. Every once in a while she'd come to school with a whole bunch of big pictures of herself in all kinds of neat clothes. She'd be leaning against a ladder, holding out a beach ball or in some other weird pose. Back then every girl I knew either wanted to be a model or a stewardess or both but Vanesa and her sister were the only ones in No. 7 that really took classes and had pictures and all.

One time I went to her house and saw the much talked of room that was just for holding toys. It did exist. I had hoped to report back to the other kids that there was no such thing but they really had a whole room filled with toys—big ones too. Brightly colored plastic toys that take up a lot of space, a make believe kitchen and a couple baby buggies. I can't remember what all kinds but there was a whole mess of toys, more than I had ever seen outside a store. They had another room just for eating where everything was blue. It was so perfect that it looked like no one had ever sat in or ate at the baby blue chairs and table in their whole life. Another time, I went to play at her house and her mother set us up on a back porch that was screened in. They had green and white striped lawn chairs and a round picnic table with an umbrella to match the chairs. To me, the whole place was like a real live Barbie doll house.

For a long time Vanesa's looks made me feel strange about myself. Her thin short hair was done up different ways all the time. Her mother would curl it and tease it and try all sorts of hairdos. Vanesa and her sister hardly ever wore the same clothes twice; at least it seemed that way to me and the other girls. She used to say that she could keep the clothes she'd modeled in and that made us all want to be models even more. There was one autumn in my life that I wore the same poncho every day because I really liked it and because it was the only one I had; they were in style that year. I wouldn't have my mother crochet me any other, though she didn't have time to anyway. This one was store bought and had lots of red in it, my favorite color. One day after lunch when I was walking toward Vanesa and a group of girls that surrounded her in the schoolyard when she said, "Here comes Little Miss Riding Poncho." I laughed with them but I never wore it again even though I had a skirt that matched it perfectly. It took tremendous effort to leave the house without the poncho when I put on that skirt.

Anyway, Vanesa's mother must have loved to dress her daughters because they strutted their stuff year round, not just at Easter time like the rest of us kids. Easter was a big deal for my brother and me. We got hats, gloves, new shoes and pastel colored outfits. Sometimes I'd even get a new pocketbook with a flower or shells behind a plastic covering on the outside. One spring my mother got me a bright yellow cape with a short sleeved dress that went underneath. I had a white straw hat and I wore it all to school the Monday after Easter. Vanesa said I looked like an egg. I told her that her new lavender coat and shoes were pretty. She was still my friend.

When I was very little and my brother wasn't even in school, my mother sewed the majority of our clothes. One time, she even made my brother an Easter suit—shirt and all. She used to make clothes for my Barbie too but when we got older and she was working a lot, she didn't have time to sew anymore. My brother could care less; he wasn't in competition with Vanesa or even her sister. He was a boy and boys didn't worry about the color of their socks or shoes or how they brushed their hair. My brother's hair was always a mess but only my mother fussed about that. My hair was very long and very wavy and too thick. My mother says that when I was little she could shape long curls with just her finger and a brush. At eleven, I would end up in tears if there wasn't any cream rinse in the house to untangle the knots in my wet matted hair. Large hairy spider like clumps of it would always form at the nape of my neck—the hardest place for me to get to and I would hate to ask for help combing it, especially my father; he showed no mercy and would pull the comb through it and always yank my head back. Almost everyone at school parted their hair down the middle. I did too but I had a widow's peak, so I would pluck out the springy black hairs to keep my hairline even like Vanesa's. She had no problem with knots because her hair was feather light and fine. She even used hair spray sometimes.

As I got older and began to demand some new clothes for the fall, my mother would take me on a shopping excursion out to one of the new "malls" somewhere downstate. I was usually allowed to have a couple of new shirts, two or three pairs of pants (after the public school allowed girls to wear pants, that is), and maybe an accessory or two like a sparkle belt, a necktie or sweater vest. Luckily for me, I had destructive feet. Shoes would never last longer than two months on me so my mother had to get me new ones throughout the year. Another lucky break I got was that my mother had a friend at work that had a niece a year older than me and every once in a while a large department store bag of hand me downs would accompany my mother home from the factory. This girl, who I never met and whose name I've long forgotten, saved me much embarrassment in my life.

Also as I got older, hair became a traumatic issue for me. Hair that was before unnoticed began to make itself oh too obvious on my arms and legs. I took to wearing long sleeved blouses or sweaters even in the summer. I wore opaque tights when everyone else, particularly Vanesa, was wearing stylish knee socks—always matching her outfit. Once I tried to shave my legs with a razor cartridge that my father had thrown away; it was a bloody mess. My mother grounded me for a week after school, until all the dark hair popped out in prickly points and most of the scabs had fallen off. When the school let us wear pants, that's all I wore. Vanesa paraded her various hemmed skirts—mini, midi and maxi. I watched in awe. We had stopped being friends by then because I was best friends with Rosy. Rosy and I had more in common because we spoke Spanish—our parents were Cuban. We both had little brothers that were pains in the butt. We were the same age and Rosy lived next door. She was darker than me and her hair was kinkier though she didn't have furry legs like me. One time when I was still friends with both of them—and very happy about it—Vanesa asked me why I was hanging around with a black girl. I told her that Rosy wasn't black, that she had a tan because she went to Florida every year in the summer. Vanesa laughed at me and began to say ugly things and show her teeth—pearly white ones (mine are yellow). I pushed her and we fought, although she fought more like a girl, pulling my hair but I was waving my fists around and getting in some good shots. We hardly drew a crowd, most everyone had gone home, but after we each knocked the other down and had run out of nasty stuff to say to each other we went our separate ways, she to her pretty new house with white aluminum siding by the park, me to my dusty backyard. I tried to build something with my father's hammer, some nails and a couple of pieces of scrap wood. Rosy looked over the fence and asked me what I was doing. I don't remember what I said but she climbed over the splintery wooden stakes to help me and we were always together after that.

LOVE AND PUNISHMENT AT THE CLERK
OF THE COUNTY COURTS OFFICE

The first weirdness is that there is a touch screen kiosk, which really isn't a kiosk but more like a mini-ATM. Customers, like me, have to "state their business with the court" before they get a number. The options are: Tickets, Taxes, Passports, Permits—and maybe one other thing like that. It just so happens I go to the Clerk of the County Courts branch office on Valentine's Day, a weird day for civic business but I need to pay our house taxes before the late penalty charge which would be a big chunk and not something we can afford. I'm not late though would be if I hadn't reminded my husband Josue about it. He tends to wait until the last minute for everything and the other reason is he's a cheap bastard and he doesn't "want to give them even one day more with his money."

Whatever, it's not a stressful thing and actually I'm grinning like a stupid because when I went down the hall to drink water I see people are getting married in a balloon-filled room with a white and red decorated four tier make-believe cake in one corner. One woman, waiting for her groom to get the car probably, is wearing a long lace dress with puffy sleeves like from the 1970s or a thrift store. There's a couple holding hands, dressed in jeans and matching black tees, with their sun-weathered faces repeated in an imprint across the front of their shirts; they stand before an official who's dressed better than they are. Along one side of the narrow room, I see a folding table with real white cake, white frosting starting to slide off the top. There are fake flowers and little palm trees too but a nice arch with white lights in the shape of bells and I can't stop smiling. I wonder if my husband will marry me again. Could I make Josue leave his job and come down here to this suburban satellite office, not even the super-busy downtown one, to get married again, renew the vows we took when were we so much younger, just for the hell of it? It doesn't take but a couple of seconds to know. Of course, he wouldn't. He'd say I already married you or why bother or something like that. Not an ounce of romance in that five-foot-seven-inch-hunk-a-man. Even though he's the one shoulda come pay this bill and not me but I did have the day off so of course that settles that. Besides I expect he'll bring home flowers and maybe my favorite dark chocolate mints. He'd better if he plans on getting lucky.

So, I'm sitting in the main waiting area, number twenty-seven. The display says fourteen; God knows how long I'll be here. I'm squirming to adjust my tailbone to the blasted hard plastic chairs. Looking around, I can tell that some people, dozing or heads bent over their phones, have been here a while. One guy steps outside just after I sit and returns five minutes later reeking, his last drag trailing. At the window furthest from me, there's a woman with a baby on her hip and another woman standing with her. The one with the baby listens hard to the clerk while the other woman translates whatever she says. Back and forth, English to Spanish, Spanish to English and all the while that baby is quiet as can be. Almost like she understands everything, so calm, her face a Buddha. Amazing.

There's a young woman with choppy mercurochrome red

hair and a bunch of piercings; she's so close to the window it looks like one of the rings could get caught in the mesh. Her voice is gravelly, straining, but it's futile because we all can hear. Everyone's business here is public. The clerk says, "That's $175. How will you be paying?"

At the counter closest to me there's an old man, in his seventies or eighties—hard to tell with white folks. This viejo might not even be that old. Mima's gonna be sixty-four this year and looks damn good. I'm hoping those genes kick in soon because I have little lines around my eyes already and I'm just thirty-five. Josue's four years older than me and likes to say he robbed the cradle. He stopped saying that when I miscarried the third time. It's been a while.

El viejito is so frail, you can see the veins all through his face. It kinda hurts to look at him. The clerk speaks loudly into the mic because the old man talks at the glass and not into the metal mesh talk-hole in the window. "Sir, please," the woman on the other side takes her pen to point to the hole but obviously el viejito can't see too good because he keeps talking to the glass. Finally, the punk girl at the counter next to him leans over and directs him to the right place, where he says, "I have a ticket I need to pay."

The clerk takes the slip he slides under the window and says, "Sir, that'll be $165 for this one. Would you like to pay for your other tickets and did you know that your license is suspended, sir?"

The viejito is confused. The black lady next to me stifles a chuckle and I just widen my eyes and bite my lip when I look her way. She is number twenty and I think I'd better not look at her again because I'll snort-laugh loud and obnoxious-like and I don't want to disrespect. But she seems like she'd like that.

"Sir, you have other outstanding tickets."

Nothing. The viejo just stares.

"Will you be paying for the other tickets, sir?"

Now I wonder if he even heard her about the license but then she asks him a question he answers right away.

"Sir, how did you get here today?"

"I drove myself." He takes out his wallet, his hand shaking a little but his long thin fingers are steady when he pulls out his license.

"Sir, you shouldn't be driving. Your license is suspended."

"It's right here."

"Your license is suspended because you have outstanding tickets and never paid."

Wow, says the lady next to me. I can't tell how old she is but she's older than me and thick and I'm shaking my head, looking down then suddenly up at the family coming in with such a ruckus, they grab my attention. They look Central American, probably Guatemaltecos. Parents, two little girls with pink and white ribbons threaded through their shiny black braids and a blank-faced teenager, pants sagging and moving like any other American teen. Passport customers. I turn back to the old guy after checking out that beautiful Buddha baby again, still serenely watching the translation show.

"I just want to pay this ticket."

"Yes, sir. But do you know that if a police officer stops you on your way home, you can be arrested."

I bet he thinks no cop will arrest a viejito like him who looks like he's made of porcelain and if you breathed on him too hard he'd shatter. Josue's as dark as this lady next to me; I'm sure he's gonna look better than me before too long.

"How much?"

She punches an oversize calculator I can see from here and says, "$373."

"How much for my license?"

"You have to pay the $373 and then take your receipt," she pulls a paper from a bin behind her, "and fill this and this out," she says pointing, "and then with these forms and your receipt from today you go to the Division of Motor Vehicles and take a written test to have your license reinstated."

The Guatemalan family is number thirty. I missed two other customers. My friend next to me is tsking and I think, there's no way this old man is gonna do all that. He probably just drives to the grocery store and back once a week, maybe church and doctors' appointments. But then he pulls out some bills, a little pile of them, and pushes them under the window. Even the clerk looks surprised. She counts, starts typing in his information and prints out a receipt and returns his change. She holds up the forms again.

"You have to fill them all out, front and back and take them with your receipt to the Division of Motor Vehicles."

"Yes, yes."

El viejo is shuffling past. The lady next to me says, "Well, all right then." He doesn't notice but I have to put my hand over my mouth to stop from laughing.

"Bless his heart," she says smiling and nodding.

The electronic tone goes off and the numbers advance by one then two. The woman with the perfectly behaved baby is gone; I missed seeing that sweetness once more. The punky chick is wrapping up. The passport girls are sharing a DS; kinda young for that but oh well, how'd I know. My neighbor's phone goes off and I remember I didn't turn down the ringer on mine. I pull it out and start playing the bird game. She's telling Betty she'll call her back.

"Those are so addicting, aren't they?" she says to me.

I agree and we compare notes when I get a text from Josue. He has sent me a photo of one of those little heart-shaped candies with the message: "I fucking love you, bitch," and I bust out laughing so hard the black lady next to me wants in and I just pass her the phone. She shrieks while tears are streaming down my face. I can't even speak.

I text him, "that's just wrong," and keep laughing and crying.

TALL, DARK

Almond-shaped eyes, blue black hair and built; he was beautiful. Me, stupid, eighteen and on my first visit to the top of the Empire State Building. One look and I was his, though he didn't know it. I followed him around the platform, him a magnet and me a quivering paper clip. Part of a heart tattoo peaked from beneath his gleaming white tee shirt. And I didn't have to hear his voice to know it was golden honey. People were crowding around, pushing with their bodies, all for the best views. New York City, hot, hazy and loud spread out below and beyond. As I reached him, he turned to smile broadly, just past me. His girl rushed up to kiss the lips I was already crying over.

OFFERINGS FOR A CAPRICIOUS GOD

The house is very neatly kept from the outside so that's why you'd notice if there was anything strange about or around it. Sitting on the corner of a long block, at the top of a hill, it's white and black with a red front door and a nice pitched roof, just two stories. It's mostly creamy white and the black isn't overwhelming. You know how too much black paint on a house can make it seem gloomy? This one's not. No porch and no trees around but the shutters are red and the windows are trimmed in black, so it really stands out. You'd look at it and say to yourself—nice house. That's why it struck me as odd that it would be a place, especially in here in the sticks of Western Pennsylvania, where offerings would be left.

So, who thinks about stuff like that, right? Well, if your father is like mine, you would too because his side of the family's totally into santería and all that black Cuban mumbo jumbo. Even though I don't follow it, we Cubans have a saying, no creo, pero lo respeto—I don't believe in it but I respect it. Like we don't want to take any chances with it comes to gods and saints, their tricks and power.

Across from the house is a condemned Victorian, falling to pieces bit by bit. On the other corners, a weed-filled lot that students use for overflow parking on game days and across from that, a paved one belonging to the copy joint; the owners prowl their lot and will send a tow truck at the drop of a hat. So the little house is by its lonesome on that corner. There's never anyone in the entry, getting mail or on the back stoop or just looking out the window. It looks like there's no one living there except, it does, you know? It seems that there's a lot going on inside behind the thick curtains and closed blinds. Passing by, you'd might get the feeling, is something there? Someone maybe?

Anyway, you know how you always take a particular route to go to work or to get home? You do that whether driving or walking, right? Right? I mean, I don't think I'm the only one 'cause I always see the same folks, almost always, on my way coming or going. I walk, most times anyway when the weather's good enough—I don't understand how it's always freaking raining here. Never thought it would be so much different from Jersey and so different from living in a real city which I really miss now that I'm in this podunk of a nowhere town. But I had to leave. Guess it's like my father having to leave Cuba. I think about him at sixteen getting on that rickety excuse for a raft his crazy uncles Pepe and Omar built, and wonder how in the hell they made it to Florida, their first landfall toward their eventual destination "nueva yersi" as he still calls it. He said they were protected because his mother made a promise to St. Anthony and that's why he is devoted. So much so that it drove my mom to the edge. And it's probably why I applied for a job here of all places, a whole gas tank away from home.

I have to pass this house. I say I have to but, of course, I don't. Like no one said, don't take the other way or as if there is only one way, but really, why would you take the long way? So back to my point, I pass this house all the time because it's on the route that's easiest to and from work. First time I passed this house, not the very first time, you know, but the first time I saw something weird, I came up the block towards the corner and walked alongside the front of the house and noticed a gray plastic grocery bag in the flowerbed, which by the way, is bare, no flowers or bushes, just white gravel. On the grocery bag were several dog turds. Ok, so that's not weird, right? But the crap was on top of the bag, several pieces of it and the bag was on its side so the opening was closed. I thought: why would you scoop the poop if you weren't gonna follow through and get rid of it? Maybe the dog owner was a lazy-ass; maybe they just grabbed the crap off the sidewalk and left it in there because they were too grossed out to toss it into the next garbage can? I should say that this small college town has garbage cans along major intersections but this wasn't one of them. The nearest was probably a block away, at most, up near the crossroads. So, if the pooper-scooper, and this is assuming it was a decent person, wanted to do the right thing, then why wasn't this same person willing to go the extra block? Well, I couldn't help but think about this because I passed that bag and shit every day for a week and I thought, ok, if I were the dog owner I might not ordinarily go toward the garbage can or may have just come from that way so why backtrack? Maybe that street's too busy and it'd be dangerous with a dog that might run out into traffic (that was quite a load so it had to be a dog big enough to pull a person).

On the sixth or seventh day of passing this corner, this house, that decomposing pile, I thought, ay, what if's not dog shit? What if it's human and someone's pissed off at the inhabitants of the quiet little house at the top of the hill? What if someone was doing a spell, a santería job?

I got distracted from that line of thought because of torrential rains for three days when I drove to work. I can't really look at that house too much when I'm driving because it's on kind of an odd corner. There was an accident there last month and I was in the car behind the one that got hit and almost joined the party when I started to glance over at the rundown Victoria but the screeching tires and smashing plastic jolted me to attention. No more sightseeing while driving for me now.

The weather cleared—not sunny but not wet; it was cool, really pleasant to walk again. Coming home I rounded that corner (I wasn't thinking about what I'd see either—there was a fight at work and I was trying to figure out how this particular she-said-he-said evolved into I'm gonna knock you into next week you redneck asshole to which said hick responded, I'd like to see you try). I turned and right there in the flower bed was that gray plastic grocery bag—I thought it was the same one but who knows, and the shit's gone but now, next to the bag is a whole bunch of gherkins. Bright green little pickles in the flowerbed next to the bag. So I think this is definitely bizarre. I try to remember if there was any kind of ritual requiring pickles but of course, it's not like I can ask anyone about this stuff, especially not my father's people because they might think I'm returning to the fold. Nope, can't have that. I think to myself: what's the deal here? The shit's gone, bag's here, now pickles. I wonder if maybe it's not about hoodoo and maybe the person who left this just dropped the bag and broke the jar? But again, why leave this stuff here? Why not throw them out in a proper garbage?

I start trying to put the two things together. Mojones and pepinos. They're both similarly shaped—like phalluses. Now I know some people have a big problem with that word but not me. I think it's one of those shapes that you should know to recognize because they're all over and once you notice them, then I figure, you're better off knowing they're there. I see dicks all over the place. It's not like penis envy either 'cause if I want one, I know just where to get one. Ever notice how much food is shaped like a phallus? Don't know when I made that connection, way before the flowerbed pickles, for sure—hot dogs, sausage, freeze pops, bananas, cukes, zucchini and other stuff that may or may not look like phalluses to other people. But Freud or no, sometimes one doesn't have anything to do with another. Take ties, for instance. I mean neckties. To me, they are exterior penises; mostly men wear 'em, right? They seem preoccupied with them too, always touching or stroking them. Men with power or who want to portray power always wear them. People who want to command respect, or admiration, even women, right? Think about it.

There are times when I think I think too much, like with those offerings, you know. Like there's got to be some connection, some deep hidden meaning to any odd stuff that happens that most normal people wouldn't trouble themselves about, and by that I mean people who don't know about this other world where you have to ask permission of a trickster god who's always watching you cross the street or an ocean. Most normal people wouldn't see it, or think about why these creepy things would happen or what they mean.

I was still trying to figure it out when, within a week, fish tank gravel, neon bright blue and orange, was now dumped in the flowerbed. One day I turned that corner again and this time, there were plops of fish tank gravel—not piles, not spread out in a pattern or nothing, but fish tank gravel, which is unlike anything else, tacky with its unnatural colors surrounded by pale grass, plain dirt and scraggly weeds poking through ordinary garden gravel. Now I was bewildered but mostly kinda irked that I let something so stupid bother me because I know for damn sure there is no fish gravel in santería. Sacrificing of chickens, goats and setting out honey, candy or rum for the gods, yes; but no fish gravel or pickles. And for sure, no shit.

And then, just as I was about to go down the block, in a split second flash, I thought I saw a funky looking dude, wearing a half-red, half-black jumpsuit, topped with a matching jester's hat. He was sitting up on the roof laughing his ass off. Yup, he got me good. Shoulda known it was Eleguá, my dad's protector. Had me shaking my head, tsking and muttering his tutu prayer all the way back home.

EL CHINO Y LA RUBIA

Cuba seemed spectacular in 1950 when Lei disembarked the stinking, leaky excuse for a ship, full of his half-starving compatriots. His native country, China, had been devastated after the war, with drought, famine and unrest in the north. Lei's life had been hard there, but he was not begrudging of hard work; on the contrary, even when he labored as a mechanic's apprentice for six years without praise or encouragement, Lei still believed he would be rewarded, if not in this life then in the next. The old mechanic never let him work on the cars by himself, always correcting him or completing a job himself when Lei got close to finishing. When the time came for his apprenticeship to end, Lei reminded the mechanic of all this. The old man laughed bitterly before threatening him with a raised wrench and finally dismissing him. But Lei had been a careful observer, learning all he needed to start his own shop, and he had saved enough money. Then his mother's illness came.

Lei tried mightily to maintain balance while his mother sunk lower and lower into disease of the body and mind. She had been the talkative one; Lei was comfortable in his own company, but after her death, he found the silence in their home suffocating. All that was left was a new, though not unfamiliar sparseness, the result of the sale of everything except his pallet. Even his Mother's lacquered combs, wedding garments and cooking things were gone—the only legacy a poor widow could offer an only son. He contemplated his prospects during the mourning period and considered writing a formal letter to First Uncle in his best Cantonese, but was discouraged by the poor ink and paper Mother had left behind.

One day, Lei found four sticks of incense and took them to the ancestral hall. He kneeled before the photographs of Father, whose arched brows were like his own, Grandfather, and the icons representing the earlier generations. "What can I do in such a place?" he implored his ancestors. The only response was the heavy scented smoke before him, curling into his nostrils, causing him to cough.

While the ancestors remained mute, there were thunderous voices calling to Lei in the old stories he had heard about the island shaped like a crocodile; third and fourth hand tales because none of the tellers had ever returned. After the occupation, a few men had come back, though sometimes it was just their bones. There had been one man in a nearby village who returned with king-like riches; he ordered a banquet of delicacies, what could be found, for all his relations. Before the full moon, he collected his sons and departed on the next ship.

Then word of his mother's death reached across an ocean, a continent and a sea to Cuba, where First Uncle—the oldest of the Chan brothers (Lei's father had been the youngest)—had emigrated decades before Lei was born. Twenty-three, free of obligation but not debt (his mother's last wish was a traditional funeral), and fearful of the leadership's next move, Lei's receipt of First Uncle's money cable was the luck he'd waited for his whole life. The funds covered an excruciatingly slow passage across the Pacific then down the North American west coast and through the canal and into the sometimes sky blue, sometimes lagoon green waters of the Caribbean then north to the dark Gulf of Mexico and finally back to liquid lightness in the Florida Straits.

In Cuba, First Uncle had become a very successful entrepreneur, settling in Regla, the eastern across the bay neighbor and municipality of Havana, where there had been Chinese for over a hundred years. First Uncle had started his first business there, a cantina; then, over time, three other businesses, each larger than the next, the biggest and furthest east a soy sauce factory in Santiago that First Uncle inspected at different times every month. (This, he said, kept his employees and second wife guessing.) There was also his bodega in the Barrio Chino, the smallest on Calle Dragones but the only one that sold candied ginger crickets, a family recipe that kept the Cantonese customers returning and picking up other trinkets that they could have gotten elsewhere. First Uncle's favorite business was the bar he managed adjacent to the cantina.

First Uncle was very happy to see Lei, though he had never met him before. From the port, he took Lei directly to the upstairs apartment he would share with two of First Uncle's unmarried sons—cousins Xiang and Ning, both taller, younger and with darker skin than Lei.

"Here you must wash up before you have a good meal," said Ning, leading him to a bathroom with an immense porcelain tub. A blue tin pitcher sat next to the clawed foot. Ning handed Lei some new clothes, and Lei was glad they weren't in the awkward western style First Uncle had been wearing.

That first night in the cantina, Lei was fed comida criolla to uncomfortable fullness—steaming fried rice cooked with sprouts and vegetables, two kinds of fried plantains, some other unknown boiled viands and a platter overflowing with succulent roast pork, all washed down with small cups of a transparent drink that warmed his throat and chest.

"That's ron, nephew, Cubans' gift to the world." First Uncle lifted his cup high, swallowed deeply, then slammed it down on the table and laughed as he shook his great head. "That and Cuban women, of course!" Lei had previously only seen one photo of First Uncle, taken when he left China; it seemed impossible to him that the thin young, dark-haired man from the picture and the large fleshy man before him were the same person.

It shamed Lei that he couldn't answer most of First Uncle's questions about Guangdong, but the city had been transformed by the war; Lei's city would be unrecognizable to First Uncle. Still it surprised him to hear how aware First Uncle was of the politics in their homeland, more than Lei ever had been. First Uncle read the Chinese and Cuban-Chinese newspapers every day during the slow midafternoon siesta time. "You don't know how lucky you are to have gotten out of China before Mao and his gang sunk their fangs deeper in." Lei wasn't sure what First Uncle was talking about, but he nodded respectfully.

After a second then third bottle of the fire water First Uncle dispatched with only a little help from Lei and his cousins, Xiang and Ning began clearing the cups.

"Rest, nephew. Get some comfortable sleep in your new home." First Uncle struggled to stand. Xiang took an arm to steady his father. "Tomorrow you start your new life in paradise! Before long you will marry a fine Cuban wife and have many strong sons like mine." He laughed and stumbled a bit on his way out, a corpulent arm linked with a muscled one.

Ning patted Lei on the back and led him upstairs then through a windowless room filled with large chairs and two sofas. On one wall was a white curtain, swaying in the breeze. Ning pulled the curtain aside to reveal a small room facing the wide alley in the back of the building. Inside was a narrow cot with thick bedding on top, a tall dark wood dresser, a stand-alone oval mirror in a corner and three hooks on the wall behind it with three empty hangers.

"Cousin, this is your room." Ning opened the top drawer, pulled out a pair of pajamas and laid them on the mattress.

Lei was confused. "But cousin, where do you and Xiang sleep?"

"Oh, do not worry yourself." Ning laughed a little before gesturing to the curtain. "We have always slept in the other room. The noise and stink of the street," he screwed up his face, "it disturbs us. Xiang thinks you won't last long in here either. If you find it's too much, we can move the cot." Before Lei could thank him, Ning was gone.

Lei looked around. His own room for the first time in his life. It was small, yes, but with a window where all sorts of new city sights, smells and throbbing music reached him. He hardly slept at all that night, hungrily absorbing the comings and goings of the fast-moving and fast-talking people, focusing on everything in his line of vision from quiet and dark apartment windows to full clothes lines strewn between balconies to cars and motorcycles whose loud mufflers echoed down the narrow street to the stray dogs angrily scavenging the trash heap behind the cantina. He drank it all in until the lights lost their glow as the sun rose slowly over the rooftops. His eyelids heavy, he slept briefly, until his cousins found him atop the cot, the pajamas beneath him.

A week or so after Lei's arrival had been properly celebrated and he'd been introduced to all of the staff in the bar, cantina, and bodega, First Uncle sat him down in the bar's office and closed the door behind him. There was something important he had to say.

"Before I left, I told my brothers I would send for them if I achieved any success in this new world." First Uncle was smoking a thick, aromatic cigar. Lei blinked when he coughed a little, remembering the incense he had burned for their common ancestors.

"Lei-son, I had to work very hard for a very long time. Third brother, your father, was still a very young man when I left; neither he nor Second Brother had married yet." He took deep pulls in and short puffs out of the cigar. Lei looked at the thick fingers poking from the sleeves of the pleated white linen shirt; First Uncle had assured Lei that this was the most elegant style a businessman could wear in Cuba.

"Lei-son, it was hard, hard for a long time. I have worked in every province from here to El Oriente, as far east as you can go on this island, but I succeeded. I have nine sons, Lei! Already I am a grandfather of eight boys." First Uncle laughed, then took a few more puffs from his cigar.

"The Cantonese have helped each other here. And my good luck helped me in business." He paused to sigh and look Lei in the eyes. "So when I was ready to wire the funds to bring my brothers to the island, it was then that I learned of your father's death." First Uncle bowed his head.

Lei had been a little boy when his father was killed by an explosion in a factory on the outskirts of their home near a tributary of the Pearl River. He remembers watching his wailing mother as she pulled out her hair in clumps when the surviving and still injured co-workers gave her the news. Not long after, she lost the baby she was carrying. Lei was more distraught realizing he'd never have a playmate and companion than he was when his father died, a man who left the apartment before he woke up and arrived home after he had gone to bed.

"Then it was the occupation and it was impossible to send help." First Uncle shook his head and cursed under his breath.

"First Uncle," Lei started then bowed. "I am grateful for what you have done for me." He bowed again. Lei wanted to mention how much his mother had depended on the payments First Uncle had sent after the Japanese left, but he stopped when he heard his uncle clear his throat and curse again.

"And that scoundrel brother of mine! Can you believe he had the nerve to ask for more money a few years after he ran away?" Second Uncle had taken all the money First Uncle had given for Lei's father's funeral and disappeared. Later on, Lei's abandoned cousins had been left orphaned when their mother—who believed the family cursed—ended her life in an opium den.

"I made sure his debtors understood that I would rather cut off my arm," First Uncle gestured, sawing across his thick bicep, "than give Chengdao a Cuban quilo."

Lei's furrowed brow amused him.

"Ah, Lei-son, a Cuban quilo isn't worth much, but soon you'll see. Soon, you will have your own money." He knit his graying brows, adding, "I have an obligation with all my sons of course, but you will earn a fair income. You will work hard, just like I did." He reached across the narrow desk to rest a ringed hand on Lei's thin shoulder.

Lei was put to work washing heavy dishes, bussing tables, and eventually, helping the cook, but the customers complained about his too greasy fried rice and too dry maduros. After that, First Uncle put him at the café window, where there were only three possible orders:

Cafecito, a shot of black, sweetened Cuban café; cortadito, café mixed with a little steamed milk; and colado, more milk with less café.

Ning and Xiang spoke Spanish easily with the customers, so Lei asked them to teach him the language. Once he had learned enough, Lei began to take orders at the four tables in the cantina. He would listen carefully, repeat the orders back to the customers in his poor Spanish, then write them down in the little Mandarin he knew, which was the only language the cook understood. Sometimes, the patrons would laugh at his mispronunciations or approximations of Spanish, yet he never felt they were mean spirited because they laughed so heartily at themselves too. He found the customers to be a friendly people, which included the light, dark and in between skinned to the light, heavy lidded or jet almond eyed. Eventually, he improved his Spanish to the point where he understood some of the double-meanings peppering their speech.

Lei worked seven days a week. Despite the hard work and long hours, he was so grateful to have adequately-paying work in addition to his own room that it never occurred to him to ask for a day off. His cousins, however, regularly took off during the week to spend time with their women, enjoying all the lively entertainments of Havana including several casinos and nightclubs. First Uncle usually took one or both of his sons with him on his monthly visits to Santiago de Cuba, dropping them off at their mother's in Trinidad, a city with many brightly colored buildings bordering a spare plaza.

Lei had once made the trip with them to the eastern provinces during the first year after his arrival. From Havana, they drove First Uncle's vast Chevrolet down the highway called La Vía Blanca. They first passed through the suburbs spreading out from the capital. The further out they drove, the more space there was between the buildings, until the landscape was made up of small grassy hills and pasture dotted with cows. It had been so long since Lei had seen so green a countryside.

It was in the cantina that he first saw her. She was with another, older, less pretty girl. Golden brown waves styled to frame a symmetrical face set with clear blue eyes and full lips, Lei could not help himself from looking at her between taking orders. Ning, who was at the counter serving them, noticed Lei's ogling and called him over in Cantonese, telling him to go for it.

"I need you to switch with me." Ning handed him his pad, adding in Spanish, "I'm going to take a break so you finish taking these fine young ladies' order, cousin."

The girls giggled. "Someone told us the buñuelos here are very good," the exotic beauty said, titling her head, waiting for him.

But nothing escaped his open mouth. He started sweating and his hands shook.

"Do you understand Spanish, chino?" the other girl, dull brown hair, irregular, blinking eyes and uneven teeth, asked. "Eh, chinito? No español?"

"Stop it, niña, don't be rude," said the soon-to-be love of his life with a naturalness that amazed him, then electrified him as she reached across the counter to touch his forearm. "My sister has no education."

Lei took in a sharp breath before finally answering. "Perdoname, señorita," he spoke slowly, deliberately articulating each word but still unable to pronounce the r in each as he held her gaze. "It's just that in my entire life I have never seen such an exquisite creature." Lei had learned some lines from his womanizing cousins though he thought it highly unlikely that she'd be interested. But then she smiled broadly in response. Dinora Camacho, the seventh child of beleaguered campesinos with too many daughters, was indeed interested. A chino, especially a good looking one whose accent delighted her, would be a grand improvement over the cads who expected her to be a whore or desperate (which amounted to the same thing) because of her condition. She had been born with one leg shorter than the other and had walked with tremendous difficulty until she finally got special shoes that allowed her new swinging gait to appear a bit more like an affectation than a birth defect.

Being the only light-eyed, fair-haired one in her family had earned her the nickname of Rubia, a name she disliked only a little less than the hurtful Coja the neighbor boys called her. As soon as they boarded the westbound bus in Santa Clara last week, Dinora had forbidden Fernanda, her two-year older sister, from ever uttering either name. The two sisters had been sent to the capital for "proper" schooling and were itching for adventure. On the long bus ride from the interior to La Habana they had made a pact to be modern women together no matter what barriers to freedom their great aunt Matilde posed.

A widow, whose only son had died of a childhood fever, Matilde had taken in her youngest grandnieces from the countryside in order to improve their lot and "avoid the shameful poverty of el campo." The oldest sisters of the family were beyond Matilde's help since they had already been mothers two and three times over and had never even left Las Villas province.

Fernanda was considered more unmarriageable than Dinora, not just because of her plain looks but due to a nervous tick that caused her to blink uncontrollably.

After matriculating at school and familiarizing themselves with their great aunt's expectations—no slovenliness or disrespect would be tolerated and good grades would be rewarded with an allowance for clothes and incidentals—the sisters eagerly left her house for the world outside. To get their bearings, they first explored the nearby neighborhood, where they found a cantina called El Caimán. A stuffed crocodile hung over the bar, its long toothy snout open wide in greeting.

After her first meeting with Lei, Dinora started coming in to the cantina every afternoon for her favorite snack—pudín de pan. When he saw that she picked out the raisins from the bread pudding, Lei had the cook make a special version without raisins and extra almond slivers just for her.

At first, she coyly encouraged him to tell her stories of China, but Lei was still too unsteady in his Spanish to relate complete sentences without lapsing into Cantonese. Besides, he was more interested in hearing her honey voice. Lei would wipe down the counters as she told him about her "wretched old life" in the miserable countryside. She described how her father and uncles had built their bohio, something that sounded very much like a hut to Lei. Dinora said they had constructed it with pieces of her grandparents' crumbling house and topped it with a roof of palm fronds that even the heaviest of summer rains couldn't penetrate. "And a dirt floor! Can you imagine?"

Dinora had wanted Lei to call her Ñiqui, but he had trouble pronouncing that so he tried out different pet names that he had overheard Cuban men calling their women. "What, my little dove? It can't be possible." Lei raised his brows in appropriate surprise.

"Sí, truly, a dirt floor that we girls took turns sweeping with palm fronds then wetting and patting down with our bare feet."

Lei wished he could caress her feet to remove the disgraceful memory. He resolved then never to tell her his own poor history.

On another afternoon when Fernanda came along, the sisters got to talking about their mother.

"Our Mamá has the gift of insight, a special vision," Fernanda started, her lids fluttering. She had ordered the arroz con leche while Dinora was enjoying her usual. After a few spoonfuls, Lei noticed that she had a little drop of syrup at the corner of her mouth; he wanted to lick it clean.

"She can see something very far away. Like when she knew tía Matilde was sick even before we told her. Isn't that right, Ñiqui?"

"Oh, yes, that's true," Dinora agreed; her pink tongue flicked over her lips, removing the syrup.

"Querida, do you want some more?" Lei asked.

"Ay, you spoil me so!" Dinora abruptly raised a shoulder and titled her head, causing some hair to fall over part of her face while exposing the side of delicate neck. Lei took a deep breath while Fernanda kept on bragging about their mother's "gift" and how handy it was for animal husbandry.

Finally, Dinora changed the subject, talking about the new American film showing at the cinema en El Vedado, an upscale area of the capital.

"We plan on going Saturday afternoon." Fernanda interjected quickly, as if to avoid losing her nerve. "You should come and maybe your cousin Ning too?" Fernanda's cheeks flushed as her eyes did their dance.

Both Lei and Dinora chuckled, but then there was a long pause.

Fernanda broke the quiet, "What do you say, ooh…I don't even know your proper name?"

Lei thought a moment to consider the name he'd like to be called; he knew that many Cantonese took Spanish first names.

"Paco," he said with ease, savoring its strength. "Paco Lei at your service, señoritas."

Dinora's face beamed when she saw Lei in the theatre lobby.

"You came!" She rushed up to him as best as she could without tripping over her oversized shoe and kissed his cheek. Their first kiss.

Fernanda bit her thin lower lip when she saw he was alone. Her eyelids trembled as she asked, "And your cousin? He's not coming?"

"So sorry, so sorry. He couldn't."

Fernanda made clicking sounds with her saliva as she walked away. Dinora shyly took Lei's hand in hers. "Don't pay her any mind," she said, still smiling. "We'll have a good time. Come on."

After Lei paid for their tickets, she led him through the lobby and into the semi-darkness.

There were plenty of empty rows, but Dinora wanted to

be in the very center. Lei didn't care that he didn't understand much of the dialog, or was unable to focus on the subtitles because he was holding her hand. He tried not to stare; this was the closest he'd ever been to her. Dinora was absorbed by the moving images on the screen. Occasionally she would make cooing sounds whenever the overdressed lovers embraced or kissed. One of the scenes made her laugh and she turned to him to share the amusement.

"Do you like it, Paco?"

He smiled broadly, nodding. "Mucho," was all he needed to say.

Later as they walked toward the bus stop—Fernanda trailing dejectedly behind—Dinora went on and on about the most "simpatico" scenes in the movie. He watched her animated face while trying to guide her feet, lest she take a misstep and even worried that her sister would trip in the high-heeled and surprisingly narrow shoes that made him think of the very old Chinese women with bound feet.

Fernanda caught up with them. "I'm going to get ice cream, Ñiqui. What do you say, chino?"

"Oye, don't call him that!"

Dinora was defending him. He liked that.

"No matter, no matter," he said smiling. He was unoffended by the proverbial Cuban nickname for an Asian.

"You see? He doesn't care." Fernanda tapped him on the shoulder. "Vamos!" she cried out.

After the ice cream, they walked to catch the evening launch across the bay to Regla. They had to pass by the cantina on the way. Fernanda looked in to see if Ning was at the counter. He wasn't. "I think I'll head back to Matilde's now," she said. "Chino, you make sure to walk my sister all the way to the apartment, you understand?"

"Sí, claro que sí!" He answered before Fernanda turned away from them.

The two of them went inside and sat at a corner table. Ning saw them as he returned from the kitchen and prepared their cafecito. When he brought the beverages over to their table, Dinora said, "My sister was looking for you."

"What a shame," Ning raised an eyebrow that only Lei caught. Then he walked back behind the counter.

"Mi cielo," Lei said quietly into her ear, "it's late. Are you tired?"

She sighed a little and titled her head toward his face. He kissed her cheek. Their second kiss.

Matilde was waiting for them at the window when they got to the apartment.

"Tía, what are you doing there?" Dinora called out, startled.

"What are *you* doing there?" Matilde leaned out, her massive breasts hanging over the window sill.

"Me? I am being walked home by my good friend Lei. He works at la cantina near the corner of Consuelo." She stepped aside into the light. "Don't you trust that I know how to take good care of myself?"

Lei wondered how he went from being her good friend to her taking good care of herself.

"Do you think coming home at this hour with that Chinaman is good?" Matilde's wildly gesticulating upper body was imposing; the skin under her arms flapped and her breasts swayed.

"Tía, look, this young man is from the neighborhood. He walked us all the way home."

"Your sister Fernanda has been home an hour already. What the devil were you doing all this time?"

Lei didn't think this was going to end well but he had no idea how to resolve it.

"Ay, that one didn't want café." Dinora was trying to be dismissive, turning to Lei with alarm in her eyes before looking up again. "Tía, por favor. Leave it alone," she said. Turning back, she wished him a good night with a wink as she lumbered her way up the stairs.

Lei dared not walk near, but made it a point to call out to the perspiring matron illuminated by the street light. "Buenas noches, señora. Paco Lei . . ." But Matilde had already shut the window before he could finish, "at your service."

Their third kiss was prompted by another campo story Dinora told him one afternoon at the cantina. "Papá has been working in the cane fields since he was seven," she began. Her usually sunny demeanor became solemn. "My two brothers too." Little creases formed on her pale forehead.

Lei had heard First Uncle tell of the back-breaking labor in the cane that he and so many of his compatriots had performed during their early years in Cuba. First Uncle had described the snakes slithering away from the burning fields and pitch smoke choking the workers as flames lit the night. He said he made a promise to himself never to allow his progeny to cultivate anything other than a kitchen garden.

"All my uncles and grandfathers, all of them worked the cane. We have always been poor guajiros. Tía Matilde escaped that life by marrying the minister's son who was studying in the capital." She bit her lip a moment then continued. "My mother's father was an oxcart driver, a carretero, you know? Just like the song. 'Yo trabajo sin reposo,'" she sang. "That part is true; they work without rest. But the part 'en el campo vivo bien'—that's a lie. Nobody in el campo lives well." Her nostrils flared a little. "Papá almost lost his life one time when a co-worker's machete flew off its handle and hit him just behind the jugular."

Lei recalled the factory workers telling his mother about flying body parts. He looked into Dinora's eyes. They were like crystal blue pools.

"Can you imagine the blood?"

He wished to catch her first tear before it dropped.

"I was thirteen. But I was the only one who could change his bandage; neither mamá nor any of my sisters could stand the sight of it."

He took her hands in his as she sighed deeply. Softly he said, "Pobrecita angel." Then he gently guided her face towards his, the counter an awkward but not insurmountable obstacle. "Mi amor," he said while looking at her parting lips, "I don't like to know that you or your family have suffered." Her tears salted their third kiss.

Lei watched his eldest Gabriel board what passed for a raft that made the decrepit dinghies on the stinking, overcrowded Chinese ship he took so many years ago look like millionaires' yachts. How had forty-five years passed as if in a dream, Lei wondered to himself? Floating in petrol-slicked waters all around his son and three friends were detritus, palm fronds, bits of plastic, sea grasses and coconut husks. Lei could understand his leaving; the situation, the so-called "special period" they were enduring was almost worse than the famine he had left in China. Xiang's covert garden supplemented their families' rations and produced enough scallions and cabbage for the fried rice they sold clandestinely at the bodega on Dragones Street, the only business of First Uncle's left.

"Adiós," Gabriel raised an arm while holding himself steady with the other. "I'll send word back when we get to La Yuma."

Lei couldn't think of what to say. This handsome first son with his mother's light eyes had been born in the second year of the revolution, three years after he married Dinora. A year later came Roberto, the one who looked most like him. By then the spinster Fernanda had returned to el campo to teach in the literacy campaign. First Uncle had died despondently during those early, turbulent years; he was convinced his liver failed by having to absorb the bitterness of watching all his businesses appropriated by the new so-called people's government. The only exceptions were those in the barrio chino—it was said that Fidel had a Cuban Cantonese mistress.

For years Xiang cooked and let Lei run the store since the grandnephews were budding revolutionaries and had no interest in anything Chinese. To keep the large apartment in Regla when properties were seized, Lei and Dinora moved in with the increasingly senile Matilde who lived to be 102; the old woman got to hold her great grandnephews, both of whom she called Chinito, though clearly, one wasn't.

Perhaps the biggest disappointment Lei bore was when Dinora lost interest in sleeping with him after Roberto was born. He had respected the traditional new mothers' forty day rest period after giving birth, but on the forty-first day, Dinora announced that she would not be returning to their bed. They were like brother and sister after that; not uncordial nor indifferent, just familial and obligated to each other. He was discreet when taking lovers. She remained attractive into her fifties and actually got more agile as she aged, walking with only a slight swing.

Dinora was one of the first to apply for an elder's visa to visit her sisters in el norte. Fernanda had exiled herself through Mariel at the beginning of the exodus. Because things hadn't changed much in el campo since the revolution, it didn't take much convincing for Claudia to join her; she was one of the younger campo sisters whom he had met only once when she and her brood came through on their way to Mariel. In his heart he knew that Dinora's visit would be longer than the sanctioned six months. So he wasn't surprised when she decided to stay— going on five years now—to live with and care for Fernanda who was "getting crazier in the head by the day," leaving him and their two grown sons behind.

Lei thought that Fidel was very intelligent in persuading the old folks to leave the island and become another country's problem—just like with the Marielitos. Lei recalled how the people were supposed to call them all scum and criminals but he knew that most of them were just tired and disillusioned. Now the ones leaving were hungry and desperate like these balseros and his son. Launching themselves into the sea, wishing for luck beyond hope to make it to the other side, for a better way to be in the world. Lei had done so himself when he left the only homeland he had ever known and now hardly remembered.

"Good luck, my son, good luck," Lei finally called out, waving first with one arm and then more vigorously with both arms. Though tears were streaming down his face, he smiled and added, "Good luck, always. And never forget your father."

POOR AND UNHAPPY

Ofelia was too old. They would never let her. She knew it was a crazy idea, but her heart was breaking for them. Pobres infelices. Since news of the crisis at the border, Ofelia had started researching the plight of the unaccompanied children, how many of them had relatives in this country that they'd be sent to after being processed within the seventy-two hour waiting period. How Mexican children were immediately sent back because of some strange law about fronteras and that the government was considering making that apply to the Salvadoreños, Hondureños y Gualtamaltecos, too. Shocked, she read on the computer Saúl had left her about the impunity with which the gangs murderously operated and wondered about the fates of all the children who had escaped but were without any family here, the children whose parents had taken the unbelievable risk of putting their most precious thing on buses or on the precarious tops of trains to ride for interminable hours, all sent with the expectation of American compassion and generosity awaiting their beloved babies. She would never be allowed to help, but maybe her daughter, Zoila could; they would surely approve her because she had a good job and was still young enough.

She was in her kitchen carefully preparing the café for when Zoila arrived. It was her only request, so Ofelia wanted it to be fresh. She used to cook all the dishes Zoila had liked as a child, but after arguments over her refusal to eat any of it and Ofelia's having to throw out all the extra food afterwards, they settled into a routine of coffee only on their Sundays. Ofelia had so loved to cook—it was her pleasure and release. She was famous for her congrí (with red beans like her mother used to make), boliche (Saúl said only she could tenderize the roast beyond belief) and plátanos tentación (the children had especially loved the sticky sweetness).

Sundays used to be when the extended family gathered along the long table to eat, gossip, tease, laugh, and finally, relax. However, Ofelia's dinner table's leaves had long been packed away, and the recent images on the television of the children crossing the border pulled tears out of her eyes, especially after the break with Saúl and his family. Her daughter-in-law had called her an outlaw, to her face, then they took her two, so precious, so hoped-for grandchildren all the way to California where Saúl's wife Sally—who had changed her name from the "old-fashioned" Soledad—had her parents. La Sally who called herself a "California Cuban" had originally gone to study in Nueva York to get away from her family, but now she wanted to return to them because of the children. The children, Ofelia's only nietos, a boy and a girl, born in the same order as her own had come to light. They named the boy Joshua, a name she couldn't pronounce and almost as absurd as the girl's Bella which, she reasoned, if they were going to insist one call her "Bela" then they shouldn't have used the Spanish spelling. Besides that, calling one's own child Beautiful was arrogant. And so American. The children would probably never learn Spanish.

How did it happen that a mother brings a child into the world, a son no less, nurtures, loves, attends to his every need for years, so many years, only to have that child, once grown, independent, a father himself, cut her off so completely? It still boggled her mind but she was urged to get over it. That's what Zoila said after she tired of hearing her complaints, "There's nothing you can do about it so just get over it."

Zoila had no children and, at the moment, no husband. When Ofelia asked her if she would ever want a child, she had answered ridiculously, "My business is my baby" and then added that her success was her great "reward" for her hard work. Ofelia had scolded her for boasting that way, but Zoila responded with the familiar, "You're too old-fashioned to understand." Anticuada, as if a mother's concern for her child would ever go out of fashion; yet another thing Ofelia would never "get" about her daughter. Like when she changed her name to Zoe, complaining that only old women were named Zoila. Ofelia told her that only the lucky ones get to be old.

Ofelia wasn't so sure about her luck now. She leaned across the nicked counter's edge; seventy-five years old and alone. It irked her to hear people say that she looked "so good" for her age or that she was fortunate that she still had her health. While she was still strong mentally and physically—she had survived the cancer and chemo, was all clear now—besides the usual annoying damage associated with age, and controlled diabetes, so yes, relatively healthy, but what did it matter? What did she matter?

She glanced at the photo magnets on the refrigerator. There was the annual Christmas picture of Saúl and his children. Named for his father, Saúl had been the one she left her Cuba—and, more sadly, her own mother—for, to insure his freedom. He had repaid her sacrifice by putting up vast spaces between them.

She believed that his distance, emotional and now physical, was because of his wife. But maybe that was unfair of Ofelia to think, since she had a feeling it was really this country, a place where children's success was celebrated almost in spite of the support of family.

The first time Saúl had left her was to attend university in the north. Back then, he still called her religiously every Sunday. She in turn wrote him letters that often included prayer cards; at home, a candle to San José would remain lit until he returned safe and sound. But after graduation, he was never really home. Ofelia cleaned his room, washed his clothes and continued to cook his favorite meals, food that she and Zoila usually ended up quietly sharing. Ofelia worried about Saúl's heavy smoking, his plundering of their joint bank account, but whenever she expressed her concerns, he met them dismissively.

"Take it easy, ma. I'm a grown-ass man, ok?"

"How can I be ok? How can I take it easy when you haven't even talked to me or your sister for more than five minutes since you returned?" Ofelia placed her small frame in his way, demanding eye contact.

"What do you want me to say? How are you doing?" He made an ugly face that caused her to cringe. "I want to see my friends. I've got to stuff to do. Stop stressing me." He sidestepped her and was at the threshold, keys rattling in his hand.

"When are you coming home, Saúl?" She tried to remove the stridency from her voice.

"I'll get home when I get home." His narrowed eyes found hers for a moment before he moved into the dark hallway and then slammed the door.

She turned to the window over the sink; it was a bright,

already hot day. The maple in her view always turned vermillion in the fall, a reminder of when Saúl had left for good. Blessedly, Zoila was still nearby. Ofelia had been relieved when she decided to commute to the local college, especially since she was starting to get so thin and even more sullen than when her father died. Every night, Ofelia had thanked God and la virgencita that Zoila was on the right path, never any trouble, getting good grades, especially in mathematics, a subject her father had excelled at. But he wouldn't have stood for Zoila leaving home unmarried, and for leaving Ofelia all alone in that house with too many empty rooms, the house he had sacrificed his life for.

"El pobre Saúl." She had been fortunate to have had such a good man, a man who worked so hard for his family. Any time Ofelia admonished him for doing so much overtime, realizing later that she was predicting his death when she said so much work would kill him, he used to say that it was his "duty as a man" to provide everything for his family: "One never knows what will happen tomorrow." And it was just like that; an aneurysm in his brain exploded and he was gone. She bit her lip remembering his ashen, serene face in the coffin. Maybe it was a blessing that he didn't get to see what kind of adults his children turned out to be.

After her grief had evolved from sobbing fits and shuddering sighs to a silent, resigned sadness, Ofelia fixed her energies on Zoila and Saúlito. But there was no way to recover the sense of completeness when they had all four been together as a family. The house truly was a home then. Those years, even the difficult ones right after their arrival, when the children were babies and she was watching hers and her sister-in-law's three little ones, Saúl in the maintenance job at the toxic refinery near Elizabeth and all of them living in a little two story-two family that had once been the stable for the big house in the front, she could now call those years good because they had all been together. She and Saúl had embraced the struggle because they knew that at least in this country whatever they attained would be for the benefit of their children. But maybe they were wrong to come or maybe they hadn't factored in what the costs would be if their children did not understand them, if their children could not feel about things the way they did? These questions busied her mind and led her to focus again on her son.

She drifted from the kitchen to the living room and clicked on the television before lowering herself into the couch cushions. The news came on with its distinctive music that brought her to attention; it was full of those children crossing the border, as it had been for the last few weeks, especially on the Spanish language networks. Ofelia was consumed by their stories. She imagined their names, which would certainly be deferential to faith and culture—the Marías, Jesúses, or Josés. On the television screen, they appeared intact, but close-ups revealed their dark, frightened eyes. They reminded her of the balseros' drawn faces pressed against chain link fences in Key West; just months before he died, Saúl had flown to Miami to retrieve a nephew and his family but the cold was too much for them and they settled down in West Florida. Ofelia grew to dread the cold too but she could never leave New Jersey because of her children ... her daughter.

Zoila came in, carrying some packages of food. She rushed past without so much as "hi" and asked chidingly, "Ay, ma, why are you watching that? It's so depressing; for God's sake, change it."

"Hola, hija," Ofelia said, titling her face up for a kiss. Zoila's insipid peck reminded her of the grandchildren's. "It is terrible, Zoila, just horrible. Little ones as young as three coming by themselves! Can you imagine the heartbreak of the mother who sent him?" She sighed loudly.

Zoila moved her packages to one hand so she could pick up the remote. She changed the channel to one of the pseudo-courtroom shows, but to Ofelia's chagrin the judge was listening to an immigration case. She shook her head and asked Zoila to check a utility bill splayed out on the kitchen table that seemed unusually high. They never ate together, even though the cooked food was always warm when Zolia brought it. Today it was an aromatic whole roasted chicken, tied up and glistening in its plastic domed container.

"Won't you please take half with you, mija? I couldn't eat that much in a month; it will go bad," she called out to Zoila, now arranging groceries in the kitchen.

"No, ma, I got one for myself. I'll eat from it all week—after I cut it up the first day, I'll make chicken salad for lunch and stir fry is good with the white meat."

Ofelia doubted Zoila ate even a quarter of the bird because she was thinner than she'd ever seen her, her face so drawn that not even the caked-on makeup she was wearing hid the deep circles under her darkly-lashed green eyes. This wisp of a daughter who had once nursed so greedily was now as dried up as Ofelia's own remaining breast. And that "ma" grated on her worse than the mispronounced mamá. She had always spoken to her children in Spanish, even when they would only respond in English. It wasn't until Zoila needed her help with some translation for a South American client that she returned to responding in Spanish. But Saúl never did.

"Mija," Ofelia surprised herself when she asked, "Would you consider sponsoring one of those Central American children?" She had prepared herself to broach the subject by investigating the Catholic Services online; once again they were helping refugees just as they had helped her little family when they first arrived so many years ago. They had given Saúl a suit, warm clothes for her and Saúlito, only two years old at the time. Saúl was so grateful for the plane tickets to el norte that he didn't even want to accept the money they offered but Ofelia urged him to, pointing at her growing belly. More out of gratitude than tradition, Ofelia registered her family at St. Joseph's as soon as they were settled into their first apartment in Union City; she even re-baptized Saúl there once Zoila was christened and with the same godparents too, Saúl's brother Pepe and his wife Yolanda, the ones who had sponsored them and made it possible for them to leave behind the fear and hunger of Castro's communism.

"What!?" Zoila's face actually caught some color. Her hands were gesticulating awkwardly long after her mouth finally closed. "What are you talking about? Ma, are you serious? You're asking me to take care of one of those illegals?"

Ofelia's face slowly shifted after a moment of shame at the way some television audience members in the courtroom protested and wanted to turn away the beleaguered family seeking asylum, just like the protestors in California blocking the buses of children seeking safe harbor. Didn't people understand that these children had witnessed inconceivable violence, endured intolerable fear, that their very lives depended on their being sent far away, separated from their families? Why had so many

Americans said such ugly things about these poor innocents? Why had Zoila called them illegal?

"Mama, will you please tell me what is going on with you?" Zoila turned off the television and came closer. Ofelia noticed the fine lines at the edges of her almost forty-year-old daughter's eyes. She was light-skinned like her father, even lighter than her brother. She thought it a shame that neither one of her children had inherited her once healthy caramel color that had faded now with age.

Zoila took a seat next to her on the sofa. Her elegantly manicured nails were combing the tops of her thin, jean-covered thighs. Ofelia knew there would be an interrogation. Her daughter had tried to switch their roles last spring after she fell on the curb, face first, and almost broke her jaw. Zoila had thought her feeble, doddering, when in reality it was just that her feet got tangled in a loose plastic bag that the wind swirled into her path.

"Tell me what is going on with you, ma." The fine lines around her eyes were more heavily creased now. It pained Ofelia to see how much she'd aged in the last few years after her divorce from that odious individual. Pobrecita, she seemed almost used up. It occurred to Ofelia that taking care of a child would most certainly put some life back in her. As she thought it, she surprised herself again. Her plan was never for Zoila to take a child, but only to pretend to. Yet seeing her so-diminished daughter now, tears began to form. She had only wanted happiness for her children. At least Saúl had his family. Zoila needed a child; she was convinced it would save her. Ofelia wondered what words she could utter that would help her understand.

"Oye lo que te voy a decir," Ofelia began the way she began

all important statements; that imperative preface commanding attentiveness. "Those poor children don't have anybody. Do you hear me? No one."

Zoila opened her mouth, but before she could speak, Ofelia halted her with a raised hand and continued.

"Listen to me. Your father and I left our country, our mothers, your father's businesses, everything we had and knew to come here. No language, no money, nothing except your tios, Yolanda y Pepe, who didn't have a lot either. But they sponsored us; you are here and alive because someone helped us."

Zoila was the one crying now, and hard.

PATRON SAINTS

Abuelita is the reason they left Cuba. Years before, she had climbed over the fence into the Peruvian Embassy, ending up in Costa Rica, where her husband Chago claimed her and brought her to Miami. It seemed to Mireya that Abuelita had been in la Yuma forever, or at least since Mima was still young. Abuelita had started coming to visit when Miguel Angel was born, two and a half years before her. Mireya was nothing like her brother because their fathers were different, and for this, she was glad. While they shared their mother's last name, García, that might have been the only thing. Mima had told them once that children belong to their mother so that it didn't matter who their fathers were. Mireya sometimes wished Miguel Angel's father would appear from out of nowhere and take him away.

Like Mima, Mireya had wild hair. Mireya loved the color—light brown with streaks of gold—but because it was so unmanageable, she always wore it tied back tight covering her ears, a stiff wavy tail reluctantly protruding between her pale shoulders. Because Mireya was a girl, Mima wouldn't let her cut her hair except on la Virgen de Candelaria's saint day in February because she's supposed help it to grow more. Mireya wished she could cut it all off, like Miguel.

Mireya was born during the time when there was hardly any food in la Habana. Mima said she was healthy only because Abuelita sent money to buy whatever could be found. Abuelita had always helped, sending money every month, visiting every year when they allowed it. (Terrible were the years when the American president limited visits to only once in three years.) Mireya doesn't like to think of those hungry years, preferring to dwell on Abuelita's visits. She would sleep in Mima's room, in the big bed. Mima would take Mireya's little bed, while Miguel reluctantly gave her his and slept in a beach chair in the sala. (Abuelita called Mireya's spoiled brother el rey and of course, he acts like he is the king of the house, ruling over her and Mima.) Mireya knew they were lucky to have a nice place with two bedrooms, a kitchen, living room and a bathroom with a shower because Mima would tell them all the time how she used to have to heat the water for their baths on the one stove burner that worked. "Here I have four working burners so I don't have to wait to simmer the frijoles or make café."

Their apartment was in the Plaza de la Revolución district, where they could walk a few blocks to the plaza if there were mandatory demonstrations. The first one she could vividly remember was for Elian, the kid whose father wanted him back. Raúl is not as charismatic as Fidel so he didn't have too many, except for a really big May Day a year or so before their leaving. All three of them were squeezed together between a little tree and a wall with the slogan "Junto a Fidel y Raul—Revolucion." Some idiot tried to climb that weak thing and it broke right in half and the guy was thrown on top of a bunch of people who pushed him to the ground.

On her visits, Abuelita always brought lots of food and money—they would get to eat arroz con pollo made with real chicken, not that soy stuff from the rations—and gifts—pretty clothes, ribbons, jewelry, necklaces and bracelets with different charms, and big dangly earrings, though they weren't real, they were fantasia. Abuelita said this was what all the fashionable young girls were wearing in Miami; Mireya had to believe her because she didn't know anything about el norte or the world for that matter. Abuelita would take them for ice cream in the afternoons and make them wear their new outfits so that they all looked like the returning ones. Once, an old woman shouted from her decrepit balcony, calling them gusanos. Abuelita laughed and shouted back "Wouldn't you like to be one."

When they finally received permission to leave the island, their apartment, the place Mireya had lived almost all of her then twelve years, she was filled with sadness. Mima was so excited she almost didn't notice her daughter until the day she saw tears sliding down her face.

"Mamita, what's wrong? No crying! We're going to la Yuma!" She hugged Mireya tight while Miguel made crybaby faces behind her back. He was almost old enough to go to the military, so Abuela had paid extra money to speed up the process for their papers. Mima had never said anything about their fathers; somehow she found a way that didn't require their permission. In el norte, Mireya wouldn't have to even think about a father any more.

Mireya's last year was difficult. The girls at school were already picking on her because of the new jewelry, the only different thing she could wear to school because of the mandatory uniforms. One time, five of the poorest, most militant pioneras shoved her into a corner in the school courtyard between classes.

"You think you're hot shit with all that stuff, eh?" The first one, the tallest mulata in her grade, got in Mireya's face with her sour breath.

Then the second one, the only blonde in the school, tapped her shoulder. Her pointy teeth were weak, probably from sucking sugarcane stalks.

"Abuelita sending you toilet paper to wipe your gusano ass?"

Another one, who could have been Mireya's cousin, her freckled cheeks and pale skin just like her own, tugged at her left earring and it gave way, scratching her earlobe.

"Ah, look how cheap!" She pulled the other one off, laughing her flat ass off. "I'll do you a favor and take your cheap shit."

Then one of the two left knocked Mireya's books down while the other one pulled her silver-plated necklace with different size hearts and beads. They sauntered away while she picked up the papers and books, wiped her face and headed back to class.

Mireya knew exactly what Mima would say when she told her: "Pero hija, why would you wear that to school?"

They left on August 13, 2008, Fidel's birthday, usually a day of much celebration and speechifying but because of his illness, everyone was quiet with long faces, something rare for Cubanos. On that day, Mireya saw the inside of the José Marti Airport, though not the one where Abuelita had come through—that terminal is reserved for the tourists, even the returning Cubanos are allowed to be tourists but everybody knows they have to be treated nice because of all the money and things they bring with them.

The three of them seemed to be dragging their feet through the old terminal, a place where officials push you through the turnstiles and null your Cuban passport with a loud stamp right in front of you. That made Mima cry a little but Miguel let out a snicker at the guy, who looked almost as young as him. Mireya couldn't do anything, just hold Mima's hand and wait to leave her homeland.

Their airplane was big and small at the same time, a huge gray thing with wings outside and tightly crowded rows and narrow aisle inside. Everyone departing was crying or had red eyes, even the ones who were happy. No one came to see them because Mima told madrina to just drop them off, not to stay to witness "la tragedia" of exile.

Less than an hour after liftoff, they had arrived in Miami, only the second airport Mireya had ever seen and the size and look of it was the first shock. José Martí's was tiny compared to it and so many different kinds of people, so many of who didn't speak Spanish. That was a big surprise for them; they thought Miami was all Cuban with their language everywhere but that was only in some parts, and not where Abuelita lived.

I was just starting to get some game with the neighbor girls, got to feel up Kati and later her older sister Yanitza too. The gordita Lola from around the block let me stick it between her cheeks and later, after she was good and warmed up, I slipped right in the back. She said she wanted to save herself for her future husband, wouldn't even let me put a finger in her tota. Well, she's the one who missed out.

Almost all the boys around here are into baseball so I had the neighborhood to myself except for Charles and Armando, my wing men, scouting potential pussy. But even though my thirst for chocha was pretty intense, my hunger for el norte was insatiable. I always knew my destiny was to leave. I'd seen it over and over in the apartments, up and down either side of the street. The lucky ones left and whoever got left behind got their stuff and then the stuff the others brought back on visits.

I never liked school, was always getting into fights but hated the idea of forced labor en el campo. Mima managed to get me out of the work camp with an invented heart murmur. Like I'm some sickly pendejo. I think she was more afraid of all the pussy I'd be getting in those famously unsupervised sleeping barracks full of horny revolutionary youth. Ha! All the time she gives me the same rap: "Miguelito, my son, you have to be more cautious." She just doesn't want some little piece claiming I'm a father.

None of the boys from my barrio were going to get higher education; all of them wanted jobs in the tourism sector. Everybody does. Mima worked for the clinic administration and knew she could get me in too, but for what? It was the same with the party; if you had some pull, you got access to things but shitty things—a better job, maybe university, official titles but no power, mierda y más mierda. What future was there? Only if I could get a job in a hotel or restaurant but we didn't have any connections in tourism. So el norte was the only solution.

Ever since Abuela started visiting, she told us about la Yuma for real. She had her own car, a new, silver Camry and so did her husband, a big red Tundra truck. They had a house of their own that they didn't have to share with a thousand relatives, and the most amazing thing was that anything you wanted you could buy. Anything! Fifteen watches in every color if you felt like it; new shoes for each day of the week. Abuelita said you could go to the grocery store three times a day if you wanted to. I imagined myself making an easy transition with the girls too. I'm not ugly; my teeth are straight, I'm always the second or third tallest in class and my green eyes get me plenty of attention. While Mima was excited about eating beef for the first time in her life, I was looking forward to eating something else.

There was nothing left for you in Cuba. Even though your job and apartment were decent—two bedrooms—your son was getting close to the military age so there was no choice. Mamá sat you down, told you about life in la Yuma, but you couldn't conceive of how hard it would be in reality. How could you have imagined that it was harder than the island? You really do work like a mule. And if you don't have medical insurance, they treat you like some kind of leper when you can't pay. Even though in Cuba there wasn't much, what was there was free—a doctor within walking distance, usually a well-educated but poor individual you'd bring some fruit or crackers to when you visited. The doctors who treated you and your children had gone and come back from their "volunteer" work somewhere in Africa, Haiti or Venezuela. They knew what medicines would work beautifully but lamented with genuine pity that they were unavailable to Cubans. Lucky for you, the children never got really sick back there. It was your destiny to come here and almost die here, but that was later.

During Mamá's last visit, when you talked seriously about leaving, she said, "Hija, over there you have to work for many hours all at once. You don't get breaks like in Cuba. You can't just go off for a couple of hours like you do here." You used to show up to your job for an hour or two then leave before lunch to wait on line for whatever fresh vegetables were available. Then you'd go back to work, always bringing some little candy or gum for your co-workers. Nobody told on anyone because everyone took turns doing it, even the supervisor.

"Hija, there you have to drive. There are buses but they take too long and don't get you where you need to be."

"Me, driving?"

"Ooh, yes, but don't worry, neither Chago nor I will be teaching you." She laughed a little but you both knew she mostly meant Chago and his legendary character. "It's best to get you an instructor. And you know, before long Miguelito will be learning to drive too."

"Ay, how is that possible?"

"Hija, just fifteen years old and he can get a permit to drive you around from daybreak to dusk. At sixteen, if he passes the test, he will be permitted to drive any time, like an adult."

"He's just a child!"

"Yes, now, but not for long. And that's another thing. In la Yuma, time flies by and you don't even realize." Mamá closed her eyes and shook her head a couple of times. "Hija, over there you work and work. Yes, you make money but you have little time for anything else."

"So, what you are saying is . . . you're not encouraging me?"

"No, of course, not; I want you to come. I'm feeling my age," she said, rubbing her thighs. "I would love to have you and the children with me. It would be such a blessing." She took my hands in hers. "I'd love it but I don't want you to think for a moment that life is easy there."

"I know, Mamá. I am ready to work hard, to support myself and the children. But I also want to take care of you, Mamá. I know how hard you work."

"You think you know." This she said patting my hands: "Hija, I work five and a half days on my feet all day, sometimes up to twelve hours if the salon is busy. And I'm lucky to have the job, the clients. Las viejitas love the way I cut their hair and I have clients that are rich. They only live in Florida when it's cold up north and they give big tips."

"I could help you around the shop, wash hair, do all the cleaning, you know how nicely I can manicure . . ."

Mamá cut you off before you could finish.

"Hija mia, en el norte you have to have a license to touch anyone's hands. Don't you remember how hard I studied to pass the test?"

"True, you told me. But the matter is that I am prepared to work. Just get me there."

You think about that conversation a lot now that you've been in la Yuma for four years. You didn't hear her. You listened but didn't hear the hesitancy in her voice, the warning about the situation. You didn't know you needed more than she could give. And you didn't know she was already planning on leaving Miami. And you certainly didn't know you had a bomb ticking in your head.

Mireya got to sleep with Mima in Abuelita's extra bedroom— they had three for only two people! Miguel got one to himself; when Abuelita said he was too old to share a room, Mireya wanted to jump up and down and hug her tight but Miguel was so happy too that she stayed put and smiled widely in gratitude.

Abuelita and Chago took a few days off when they arrived. The first three days were spent visiting familia in Miami and shopping. Then there was a long day driving to Carolina del norte where they had lived for a year already. Mireya remembers those first months as stressful; it wasn't Miami where at least there were so many others like them. And it was summer so she and Miguel wouldn't start school until September. Even in a house with three sleeping rooms, a kitchen, sala/comedor and a "family" room, they couldn't help but bump into each other all the time. Mireya felt the tension between Miguel and Chago right away, though she thought Chago was trying to enter into his confidence—the only other male in the house after all. Mima was allowed to sweep up around Abuelita's salon so she was gone all day.

They weren't allowed to go outside, not even to get the mail. The backyard held no attraction for her; Abuelita's dog Pancho, the only reason she might have for going out there, died before they arrived. They didn't know any of the neighbors, all Americanos who waved hello from a distance but stayed away. The area where they lived, a sloped and wooded development (something like a barrio but new and with lots of grass lots in front of identical houses painted one of three different colors) was far from the stores and school, though there was a little park in the middle of it. Mima told them that once they started school they would make friends. Mireya didn't leave any friends behind so she wasn't missing them though she could tell that Miguel was anxious to have some.

Chago was semi-retired so he only worked very early mornings at the lechería. He always brought home different kinds of milk (she never knew there were so many and all from a real cow, not soy). Abuelita told them to be very quiet so Chago could sleep when he got home: "Put the volume on the televisor down low and avoid making a racket with the kitchen things."

Mima also implored them to behave but mostly it was Miguel who made all the noise. After weeks of shuffling around, hogging up Abuelita's computer, watching loud music videos and exploring the internet, a virus immobilized it. Mireya was horrified that he'd broken the computer, worried that they'd both be punished, but Chago fixed it before Mima and Abuelita got home. Chago told him it'd be best if didn't download anything anymore; Mireya overheard him explain how the computer was attacked by the dirty websites and that he had better stay away from them. After that, Miguel was supremely bored and remembered he could pick on her when everyone was gone. He'd bang on her door or adjoining wall, slip crude caricatures of her under the door, exaggerated pocked and pimpled faces with nappy hair she'd tear up and slip back under the door.

Mireya spent most of that time locked in the room watching TV for children, trying to learn English until Chago came home. Miguel soon tired of tormenting her and took to sleeping late every day, almost until Chago got home so she had the whole house to herself. She polished every piece of furniture and made sure all the glasses and dishes were gleamingly clean in the cabinets. She cleaned the windows, swept, passed the vacuum, straightened the pillows on the sofa. There was always plenty for her to do and with time and peace, she kept the house spotless.

Abuelita was pleased and Mima very proud; they told her she could start dinner before they got home. Always she set up the rice cooker so that all Abuelita had to do was push down the on button and it'd be ready once Mima got out of the shower. In the beginning she was given an easy task like seasoning the palomilla steaks. Mireya liked the marks the tenderizer made and filled each little indentation with sazón and layered the meat with thinly sliced onion rounds. She learned how to make a good picadillo with real ground beef. Mireya spent hours looking through an old Cuban cookbook, the only one Abuelita had—*Mi Cocina Criolla*. She couldn't believe how many dishes and specialties she had never even heard of. Abuelita said that after the revolution there wasn't much real Cuban food to be had. Mima reminded her that it only got worse after she left.

"Arroz con pollo, sin pollo y sin arroz!" Mima said and began the litany of all they didn't have: "Real Cuban bread was impossible; the bakers stole the lard so the bread was hard like a rock. And real milk? This generation only knew soy soy soy. Forget about beef . . ."

"Sí, I remember now! You told me about the time you made ropa vieja with grapefruit rinds." Abuelita laughed but Mireya got sad thinking of how hungry she had been and of how the concoction had been inedible.

I never was so utterly and completely bored in my life. Even jacking off got boring; all the photos and videos from the internet drove me wild, all free, unbelievable shit but then the damned virus. That bastard Chago let me print a few so I would stay in the room and out of trouble. Even with a dozen Spanish language channels, nothing on the TV interested me. Chago said that Abuela had blocked the sex channels because she didn't want to fill my head with filth. I think he's the one doesn't want to share.

I wasn't in a hurry to learn English because I knew I'd be forced to in school. In Cuba, I was obligated to go to school, but Mima didn't ask me where I went afterwards as long as I was home when whatever miserable meal she could make was ready. I had visited the roofs of the tallest apartment buildings around the plaza, even the one with el Che on the side. Most of them didn't have working elevators so I'd challenge my boys to race to the top. My long legs would be aching by the thirteenth floor but I always came in first.

In that new, pretty house, I was like a prisoner. In Cuba I could roam the streets, catch a ride to Vedado or La Rampa to see if I could charm some foreigners, trying to earn some cucs by taking their photo, carrying their bags, showing them around. A lot of those single women were young looking even though they were old and nasty; I found out the hard way. There was one, she never took off her bra, probably didn't want to show me her droopy tetas. After I got her good, she called me her niño and asked if I'd bring a couple of my friends next time. I lit out of her room at the Nacional, running down the stairs when I saw the militares coming towards me in the corridor but I outran them. I wasn't about to become a jinetero or a pimp.

Life in this Carolina was dull beyond tedium. One monotonous day after another. I had nothing to do, nowhere to go and all the crushing time of day after day. I was only permitted to go in the fenced in backyard—there was nothing to do there either, just scraggly grass, wilting flowers in plastic pots, a lone pathetic tree, a big grill and a shed housing Chago's motorcycle. That pendejo doesn't even ride it because Abuela doesn't like it. I had driven one that Charles and his older brother put together from parts they had been buying, stealing, finding and saving for years; they called it Frankenstein. After Charles' brother was sent to La Isla de la Juventud, Charles had a heyday with it and almost killed himself. Me and him stole gas from any cars we saw that were vulnerable; most had jerry-rigged the tanks to open only from the trunk. Whenever we could get enough gas, we'd fly down to the malecón and take turns giving girls rides in hopes of some action. There was always rum and good music down there and I may not be the best dancer but I surely do love reggaeton; as a matter of fact, I'd like to shake the hand of the genius who made humping and grinding in public popular.

So I got to thinking of Frankenstein and that moto in the shed all polished and hardly used and I began inventing a plan. I had to get Meya to cooperate so that meant I needed to change my ways with her. La pobre, she has Mima's bad skin and her body is in between so she doesn't look like a little girl or like a grown one yet, just shapeless. I needed to get her on my side, little bitch is always watching though she doesn't say anything to Mima. Sometimes I wished she would say something about me so I had a good reason to thrash her. But nothing; she just stares, her blank eyes don't say anything either. I had an idea how I was gonna do it. It'd take a little time but shit, that's all I had.

You didn't know what to expect. In Miami, or in Carolina del norte. There was so much you didn't even know, like being completely and obsessively dependent on your mother, and for much longer than you would have ever thought.

What you did expect was to get to work right away—point me to it, you said. They gave you a broom and you were sweeping up as soon as the clients were removing their behinds from the chairs. Maybe a little too quickly, the redhead gringa-looking Boricua said. You were nothing if not pleasant, downright appeasing. Mamá didn't always look too happy at the salon, like maybe she had second thoughts about leaving Miami—it was Chago's idea because his compadre got him the job and there were plenty of cheap new houses. Mamá had to leave all her good clients and start over in the salons tucked inside the big big store that sold everything. You couldn't believe the size of it—bank, optometrist, photographer, mechanics, grocery store, clothes store, garden store, all of it in inside a giant building taking up a city block. Mamá laughed at you when a bird shit on your head, inside the store!

"Buena suerte," she said, silly in her enjoyment. "Good luck on this your first day!"

But how was it possible that this place even had birds flying about? Were they for sale?

"No, mija. They fly in the doors when people come in. I've been here almost a year and have never seen anyone get caught. Truly, you are lucky, Aida."

You thought maybe you could be lucky. You liked the hills and tall trees you rode by as Mamá drove you to and from the salon. You paid close attention to the conversations of the clients—you'd never met Mejicanas before and now there were at least two new ones walking in each day. The Boricua redhead translated most of the time, though you were proud that Mamá could speak English, so nicely, you thought. There was a Dominicana with beautiful long black hair, like an India; you could not fathom why in the world she'd cut it off to donate it. And you with your scraggly hair that not even the most expensive conditioners could improve. Oh, what you would have given for that waterfall of hair! Later when your head was shaved, the hospital loaned you an auburn wig with highlights styled into a bob that would have made you look sexy if you hadn't been so pallid and terrified. But that was later.

The first three months you were fattened up. You tried everything you were offered and everything tasted delicious. How could you decide what you liked best when your taste buds were so orgasmicaly overloaded? Mamá loved feeding you too.

"Mira, mamita, try this. It's hayaca." She gives you this pudgy rectangle wrapped in banana leaves. "It's like Cuban tamales but with chicken and rice inside. This is from Nancy's mom; she comes every summer to visit from Caracas and makes them from scratch. Qué rico, eh?"

You agreed. You liked the Puerto Rican pasteles too; both the ones made from yuca and also the ones made from plátano. You ate and ate and swept and cleaned; full, and fully content.

You were also delighted with Mireya's transformation in this country, keeping house and cooking and you didn't even have to tell her. Your only concern was Miguel Angel, so willful and now moody. You wished September would arrive soon so he could start school and have an outlet for his energy and capriciousness. Every night you begged him to stay out of trouble, to be quiet, to stop teasing Mireya. Every night he asks you, what am I supposed to do all day, Ma? And every suggestion you make— learn English, read the Spanish newspaper, watch a movie, water Abuelita's flowers? No, no, no, no, I don't want to, I don't like it, I don't understand, I'm not going to. You sigh and assure yourself, it's his age. He'll be fine once he gets to school. Tired and without further suggestions, you kiss his clear forehead, shrug and walk away. You should have listened more closely to him too.

Mireya knew her brother was up to something. She noticed he was waking up earlier, just after she had washed and put away Mima's and Abuelita's breakfast dishes. Mireya had started to make them sandwiches for lunch, mayonnaise and ketchup with turkey and Swiss for Mima and mustard, butter, ham and Swiss for Abuelita; sometimes she added some sliced some pickles.

She loved removing the bread from its plastic sleeve to push her nose into the loaf, inhaling deeply and fondling the softness. Before finally washing the cafetera—she still had difficulty throwing out the coffee grounds after only one use—she would make herself an Elena Ruth, one of the Cuban sandwiches she had had and loved in Miami. It was made up of cream cheese, turkey and strawberry jam.

She stood at the counter eating when she heard the toilet flush.

"What's up, Meya," Miguel surprised her with a smile and upon seeing it, Mireya understood that he had to be desperate.

She nodded in recognition.

"Any café left?" He knew there always was. She nodded again. He sipped to taste then put the mug in the microwave. Usually he didn't eat anything until later; he complained that everyone was fat in this country, especially all the family— Abuelita's brother was and his wife, their adult children, even the little cousins. Mireya had probably gained a little weight but she couldn't tell because she had all new clothes.

Miguel opened the fridge and considered all the choices, but closed the door without selecting anything. Then he watched her watching TV. A red puppet was talking to an orange bug-eyed fish. Next there was a wiry man clowning around, awkwardly pulling on and off his patched vest. A little girl stepped into the frame to help him and he did likewise with her colorful vest. Mireya had absorbed much from this show in particular, and made it a point to watch every day except Sundays when there were men and women in suits talking talking talking. She understood the skit on now was about helping and cooperation. She understood the word cooperate, coperar; in Cuba they all had to because if not there were consequences.

She forgot her brother was there until he plopped down loudly on the faux-leather couch then sighed deeply. "Meya, I don't know how you can watch this shit," his frustration was palpable in his expression, his tapping foot, the way he ran his hand from his forehead back over to the top of his now unruly head of hair.

She considered before quietly answering, "I want to learn English."

It looked to her that he was considering her answer before he offered, "Wouldn't it be better if you could learn from real people? Not this comemierda baby stuff!"

There it was. He wanted to go out. She understood, but wasn't in the least interested in the outside yet. She had the cookbook, a kitchen full of wonderful new appliances and gadgets, including a refrigerator and pantry packed with more food in one place than she had seen in her whole life. The television offered endless entertainment though she deliberately steered away from the Spanish channels during the day; there was plenty of it at night with the noticias and novelas. She watched Miguel's face contort, waiting for her to respond.

"What is it that you want?" Now she was the one sighing deeply.

"Ay, mi hermana, what is it that I don't want? I want to get the hell out of here, see something, go somewhere." He stood up and over her. "Come with me." He took her forearm into his right hand, gently squeezing. "Come, let me show you something. We're not going to get into trouble."

Mireya was certain they would; she was both curious and scared as they made their way out the sliding glass door into the yard. The contrast from air conditioning to fresh, grass scented air caused her to take deep, eager breaths. This outside was so clean compared to Cuba and even Miami; no smoke, exhaust or grime lingering in the breeze. She smiled without realizing it.

"You see? It's good to leave the cage, verdad?"

Undoubtedly, it was but she couldn't, wouldn't say so.

"Come over here," he said walking toward the downward sloping corner of the yard. "Look over there, see that?" He waved her closer. "That's the little park we drive by on the way here."

Mireya wondered why it was always empty when they passed it on Sundays after going to the grocery store and any other errands Abuelita had. When she asked about it, Abuelita commented that many Americanos went to church on Sundays. And there were so many different churches too; on one street near the center of the town, there were five different denominations. Mireya had only heard of Baptists and Catholics in Cuba and had only been to the bleached white church on the hill at the top of Compostela twice, once when she was baptized and then when Abuelita came to visit the church because that's where Mima had been baptized. It was pretty, but Mireya was more interested in the sprawling cemetery city where her grandfather was buried. He lay in a tomb for soldiers because he had fought and died in the Congo, leaving Abuelita alone with baby Mima. There were so many fascinating statues and elaborate mausoleums, plot after plot with two or more vaults and osarios. Abuelita said that she could never find her father's family plot even though she checked the record books for years before she left. Mireya loved accompanying her mother to grandfather's tomb on his birthdays. Sometimes she would explore nearby when Mima got too sentimental and wanted only to sit on the bench in front of the monument for soldiers.

Miguel started back toward her, his impatience getting the better of him.

"Come on."

"What is it?"

"Ésto! Look down there. See? The park? Let's go down there. It's not far. We don't even have to take the street, see?" He was pointing to the wide easement behind the houses provided by a pitiable creek running downhill past the park until it disappeared underground by the woods.

Mireya suddenly wanted to see if there were fish or toads like on a nature show. "What do you want to do?"

He must have noticed a change in her expression because he smiled at her. "Vamos, chica. Let's go. I'll help you over the fence."

Everything after that moment seemed to pass over her like waves. First there was the accident. That knocked them all down. There was no cemetery or funeral, no place to go to grieve. Chago's remains came home in a pewter urn they had to look at every day because it was on top of the shelving unit where the big TV sat. Abuelita was so depressed, it was as if she was sleep walking all the time. Mima went crazy trying to bring her back but before long they had to return to work. Mireya just kept cleaning and cooking while Miguel spent six weeks in bed. Mima would help him to the bathroom in the mornings but she hardly talked to him. His leg healed and he joined her at school. It was the first time they were together though Miguel often walked by her without any acknowledgement. But Mireya was busy keeping afloat; her first progress report with its column of A on top of B on top of A made her even happier than it did Mima, who was working steadily at the big store and hadn't gotten sick yet. That was the wave she thought would swallow her whole. But it didn't because Mireya had to become Mima's life saver.

You started getting headaches. You thought it might be the sprays and chemicals in the salon with the poor ventilation. Mamá said it took some getting used to but then you passed out, almost cracking your skull on one of the sink bowls. A moment after you fell, there was a circle of women hovering over you but with a little face washing and cola, you were just fine.

You hadn't been in this country two months when the accident happened. You blamed yourself for different things: being a bad mother, worrying too much about money, even leaving Cuba. And your mother was so devastated, so transformed by the loss, that she emptied herself. She didn't have anything left for you or the children. She never said it but you knew she blamed your son for Chago's death.

There was not enough money for a proper funeral, so your mother had him cremated and promised his family in Cuba she'd bring a part of his ashes. Your heart hurt witnessing her sadness which was only slightly diminished when you both returned to work. The hairdressers treated her more kindly; you could only visit with her on your lunch break.

Months of work and emptiness went by. Your children were in school adjusting—not surprisingly Mireya better than Miguel Angel, whose leg was a good as new. Mamá was glad you got the job cleaning in the big big store and sheepishly took the paychecks you handed over without blinking.

You were cleaning the employee break room when your

eyes seemed to flood with liquid darkness. The last thing you remembered was a large balding black man rushing to catch you as you crumbled to the floor. You awoke in the hospital where you were examined inside and out; two kinds of machines with big cave-like openings to hold your whole body. One was so quiet the music in the room obscured the machinery, while the other was loud, with banging and rattling pulses that shook you to the core. All the while there was a low tone vibrating beneath your temples; your eyes hurt and crying made it worse. After all the tests and scans and analyses, it was Mamá's turn to gather you up and put you to bed to wait.

The children were frightened, probably more for themselves than for you. You understood their fear. So many changes, so much uncertainty. In Cuba, all was certain—struggle, hunger and fear. Come to think of it, the only difference here was abundant food. They waited with you in grief for the diagnosis; it was almost like you were already dead. Mamá took off from work. After four days of whispered, fragmented conversations, blinding headaches and nightmare-filled day dreams, the doctor's office called.

I despised school by the end of my first week. English was a mystery to me and not just because I started late. I struggled even in mathematics. Geography was interesting only because of the maps and places. So large a country, so vast and full of things I wanted to see. All the hispanos in the special classes with me were central americanos or mejicanos. A small group of us formed—immigrants and exiles, too young to quit school, too old to learn ABCs all over in an awful new language. It didn't take much to get used to their accents and soon enough

I was kidding around with a group of older guys, catching rides with them to the shopping center after school, trying to get girls' attention. I was desperate—I hadn't had pussy since Cuba. Before long I was commandeering this little salvadoreña, morenita with beautiful chinita eyes who gave it up early on. She was so sweet, I couldn't get enough. Magdalena, such an old fashioned name. I called her Magi. When Mima got sick, Magi suffered almost more than me. She would come over in the evenings and bring some typical dish or sweet. Mima liked her a lot, probably because I wasn't so combative anymore. That's what regular sex will do for you.

I almost never made it to school because I almost got myself killed. This was before Mima almost died; well, she did die once in the operating room. They were removing a mass that started out bean-sized in January and was fist-sized in February when they operated on her. Abuela said she was lucky they got it all out but Mima looked like hell afterwards. She had a long scar on her head that she covered with an absurd wig, but she couldn't hide the constant blinking and dragging left foot. She couldn't work too hard after what seemed like months of recovering and physical therapy.

Abuela was even more anxious than usual. She was never the same after the accident. I stayed out of the way as much as possible. I didn't even notice that Mireya's face had cleared up until I saw the school photos on the counter one night. The kitchen was empty, everyone in bed, but I wanted a drink of water. I almost couldn't recognize my own sister; her expression was new to me because she was smiling with her whole face. She was almost pretty. And, of course, doing well in school. Mima's little girl was going to be all right. I thought back to the day before all the shit happened, when we walked along the creek to the park. The sun had heated the playground equipment so that we couldn't sit or climb comfortably but we did anyway. At the top of the monkey bars we could see all the way to the mountains far off, beyond the houses, clusters of commerce strips, the tall downtown buildings shining brightly in the east. Mireya was agape but it wasn't enough for me. I wanted to see more. Nueva York or Las Vegas. I told her I'd seen Abuela's photos of these cities—big and full of excitement. She was only worried she'd get blamed for going through their things and for escaping to the park. I never worried about anything. That was the first little escape. Mireya never joined me again after that.

I decided I was going to ride that moto one way or another but when I checked the key wasn't in the ignition. Chago always left his keychain on a hook by the front door. That afternoon I waited for Chago to take his siesta and Meya was watching her stupid shows. I grabbed the whole key ring with both hands to muffle the noise and slipped outside. I tried every damn key but it wasn't there either. So I had to do the thing I didn't want to do, get friendly with Chago. I knew how to charm and Chago knew how miserable I was, so it was easy really. I just started asking stupid questions about the bike, how many miles it had, how much did it take to fill the tank, was he the first owner, did he get it here or in Miami? That got Chago going on and on to the point when he finally said, "Let's go for a ride."

"Coño, qué bueno, Chago." I was acting like an excited little kid.

"There are nice country roads here, you'll see. It's very pretty."

I didn't care about the scenery, I just wanted to go. And we did, most every afternoon when he came back from work.

Mireya was always afraid for us but I promised to beat her down if she told.

Finally, after a month of the afternoon rides, Chago let me drive a little way out where there weren't any cars. He said I was a good driver. He said I could use the bike when I got my license—fucking eighteen months away! But I was being careful with everything I said and did, trying hard to be cautious. Then it happened. He decided to let me take us back home. I was going to show him how to drive. I started out slow, enjoying the power. We were at the bottom of a long hill and I was shifting good. Chago even gave me a thumbs up. Then at the crest I looked to the bottom and I couldn't help myself. I wanted to go fast down the other side.

It went bad. I couldn't get the right gear shifted and the bike wobbled. I lost it. I was awake the whole time, super alert with hot blood pumping all through my body. We flipped and both of us were thrown; the bike zoomed in a ditch and my head was spinning. I felt like every bone in my body was broken though it ended up being just my leg and bruises everywhere. I called out to Chago but he didn't answer and I couldn't get up. A car stopped and before long I heard the siren. They asked me questions but I didn't understand shit. As they were putting me on a gurney, a cop who spoke broken Spanish showed up.

"Qué pasó?" He was standing in the way; I couldn't see Chago. He must have landed so far away from me.

"What do you think happened? Where is Chago? What happened to Chago?"

The cop was insistent and I knew I had to say Chago was driving or we'd all be in big trouble.

"He lost control."

"What is your name? Is there someone we can call?" He tried to calm me down.

"Please tell me, how is Chago? Where is Chago?"

"You mean Santiago?"

"Yes, yes, Santiago Gómez.

"Is that your father?"

"No, no. He's my grandmother's husband. Where is he?"

"I'm sorry."

"Qué? Qué pasó?"

"He's dead. I'm sorry, son."

I was sorry. So sorry. I couldn't remember the phone number or even the house number. The police got all the information they needed from Chago's license. The Spanish-speaking cop had to tell Abuela. I was taken to the hospital. Abuela's hoarse screams for him were terrible. She loved him so much she said over and over. So much she lost her mind a little.

As soon I turned sixteen in the spring, I quit school to go to work. Mima needed me to because we didn't have Chago's salary. Abuela hadn't gotten over his death, and she wasn't bringing in as much as before. Magdalena's father did construction and invited me to join him on the corner of the hardware warehouse where the men get picked up for day work. Samuel never took a job if he couldn't take me along; I was indebted to him. We worked well together; he said I learned fast. But I didn't want to be obligated to him, especially not when I started seeing other girls on the side.

With what I saved I bought myself a little two door 1999 Honda on my eighteenth birthday. I was giving Mima and Abuela at least $150 every week, sometimes more if the money was flowing. I learned enough English to get along and my leg would only bother me when the weather was cold and damp. When I got a steady construction job, Magdalena started hinting at marriage. We'd been together a couple of years already but I made sure to always use strong condoms, sometimes doubling them up. I planned on going to Las Vegas, where I heard they paid twice and sometimes three times as much as I earned now. I wasn't telling anyone until the last minute. Especially not Magdalena, so I started inventing new family obligations. "My mother needs me more now, Magi. Abuela can't pay for the house and all the expenses by herself. You understand, don't you?" Partly it was true; the tumor had grown back and Mima was going to have another operation and then more chemo.

"Yes, of course." Her black black eyes were filling. "Of course, I understand."

I had to look away. I needed to move forward.

AFTERWORD

After my first book *Marielitos, Balseros and Other Exiles* was published, a young filmmaker from Miami tracked me down for a documentary he was completing called *Cuban America*. Adelin Gasana wanted to interview me about Miami of the 1980s, a time I had chronicled in several stories; Adelin said he wanted to include my perspective on Marielitos. It took some doing but we finally scheduled a meeting some months later. He was gracious enough to meet me at my father's condo in the North end of Miami-Dade County. Adelin asked great questions and I had a good time answering—all the while papi was off to the side watching and listening. What I didn't know was that he was also in the frame; there on the wall behind me was a photo of a handsome, young immigrant smiling at the camera. When I got to see Adelin's finished product, I was fascinated by all the interviews narrating how both ordinary and extraordinary Cuban exiles transformed Miami. And I was tickled to see papi in the film with me—he could have easily added his own story of struggle in Miami, a place where he tried three different times to make a living before he was successful enough to settle there in 1974. Yet the most remarkable insight I gained from the film came from sociologist Lisandro Pérez who pointed out that in the first decade of this century, more Cubans have arrived in the U.S. than in all previous exoduses put together.

I don't know why this bit of information was astonishing to me. Maybe because having lived away from Miami for so many years, and even though a frequent visitor to it, I had taken for granted the Cuban nature of so many parts of the city. But then I remembered that during the early 2000s and up to 2007, I had had in my own family, an aunt and three cousins with their children and spouses arrive in the U.S. to start their American lives. And the fact that they didn't all stay in Miami was extremely interesting to me because of earlier exiles' reluctance to leave it, even when work was difficult to find and low-paying.

So I compiled this collection with the idea that I would focus on Cubans and Cuban Americans whose lives were outside of Miami since the first collection was dedicated to stories set, for the most part, in South Florida. In this book I wanted to include stories about the exiles that went to el norte (which to most Cubano/as, is anywhere north of Cuba, including la Florida) and decided to stay. I knew from experience that their children grew up in very different ways than their Miami cousins did. As a result, there are some Jersey girl narrators in this collection—"Other People's Homes," "Barbie Girl"; it's a voice I'm comfortable in. The narrator of "Big Difference" is a wannabe-Jersey girl who is reluctantly stuck in Miami while the narrator of "The Law of Progress" gives "thanks to God" that her family didn't move to Hialeah. And because these characters have only known the United States as their homeland, despite living in traditionally Cuban homes, their most comfortable language is English rather than Spanish and their accents tend to be more urban than Miami Cuban.

I also became interested in exploring why some left Cuba

before the revolution as the narrator contemplates doing in "Enough of Anything." And then there is Lei, who leaves his homeland of China but decides to stay in Cuba after the revolution, even through the "special period" of severe scarcity and despite his loved ones' departure. The most recently arrived characters to the U.S. in this book are Mireya, Aida and Miguel Angel from "Patron Saints." Just as many other newly arrived compatriots have done, they too live away from a Cuban enclave—all in hopes of gaining a foothold and getting ahead.

And what may come from the move toward the normalization of relations between the U.S. and Cuba will be solely determined by power-mongers if we don't listen to what the Cuban people have to say. Their voices, like those of the characters in this book, call out to us in the most Cuban of ways—oye. Listen.Listen.

ACKNOWLEDGMENTS

Where would any writer be without thoughtful, insightful first readers? I would most certainly be utterly lost without mine. For this book, I relished and relied upon the generosity of the sage feedback and enlightening comments of María Elvira Vera Tatá (mi queridísima), Kevin Meehan, Luis Martínez-Fernández, Detrachia (Tray) Neely, Rebecca Fortes, my longtime friend and literary co-conspirator, Janet Bohaç and also Esperanza Cintrón and Victor Villanueva—all writers whose work inspires and dazzles me. I was and am blessed to have had their help as well as the important sustenance I've gained from friendships with the likes of Ivonne Lamazares, Elena Pérez, Alma Alarcón, Litza Fonseca, Lisa Treviño Roy-Davis, and my treasured and much beloved Cuban Jersey girls—Iliana (Illy) Jiménez and Yolanda (Yoly) Lamela. I am eternally indebted for the unwavering faith in my work Elizabeth Clementson and Robert Lasner bestowed upon me; the depth of my gratitude is inexpressible.

A writer like me, who is an engaged parent of an active newly teen son as well as of an adult graduate student daughter, who teaches and mentors full time and who cares (admittedly, most times half-hazardly) for a house and home, absolutely requires the unquestioned support and strong back of her partner—Jorge Milanés. Mil gracias por todo, mi amor.

So many others helped in so many ways with their friendship, good humor and love—muy queridas amiguitas from work: Gabriela Rios, Wanda Raimundi-Ortiz, María Cristina (MC) Santana, Ilenia Colón. Other friends and colleagues who've always had my back include Kevin Meehan (still the relentless encourager), Anthony (Tony) Grajeda, Martha M. Marinara and Patrick and the indomitable Bonnie Murphy, Grisette Acevedo and Claire Mauer. Ahimsa Timoteo Bodhrán was and remains a continuous spring of reassuring love and support—always at the ready.

I am so grateful for my family and most especially for my parents Isabel Gaston Rodríguez and Mario Rodríguez, who first sparked my interest in stories by telling their own. Heartfelt gracias to the whole clan, las primas, los primos, both sides and those by marriage, too—you all know who you are.

Of course, gracias a Dios. And there are always santos to thank, La Caridad de Regla, San Antonio and others showed up this time besides my regulars. Next to the Infant of Prague medal that my mother hung around my neck for protection when I was a baby, there is a double-sided Our Lady of Charity and Santa Barbara medal and, even though it is not the original stone my grandmother brought for me all the way to New Jersey from Cuba, I wear an azabache—por si las moscas.